D0371031

You've connected.

danger.com

@2//Firestorm/

25 Years of Magical Reading

ALADDIN PAPERBACKS
EST. 1972

First Aladdin Paperbacks edition October 1997

Aladdin Paperbacks
An imprint of Simon & Schuster
Children's Publishing Division
1230 Avenue of the Americas
New York, NY 10020

The text of this book was set in 10.5 point Sabon.

Printed and bound in the United States of America

10 9 8 7 6 5 4 3 2 1

Library of Congress Cataloging-in-Publication Data
Cray, Jordan.
Firestorm / by Jordan Cray. — 1st Aladdin Paperbacks ed.
p.   cm. — (danger.com)
Summary: When fifteen-year-old Randy Kincaid accidentally
logs on to an Internet chat room and discovers a fanatical group
that he thinks may be responsible for a series of bombings, his
life in Bunnington Beach, Florida, quickly moves from boring to
endangered.
ISBN 0-689-81431-3 (pbk.)
[1. Internet (Computer network)—Fiction. 2. Computers—
Fiction. 3. Terrorism—Fiction. I. Title. II. Series.
PZ7.C85955Fi   1997
[Fic]—dc21   96-37898
CIP   AC

danger.com

@2//Firestorm/

by
jordan.cray

Aladdin Paperbacks

//prologue

He pulled up across the road and parked away from the streetlight. He turned up the radio. They were playing music he liked, for once. American pop from the early sixties, Frankie Valli, "Walk Like a Man." Sure, the guy sounded like a chipmunk with his tail caught in a vise, but he could sing.

His eyes roamed over the diner. It was a dump now. Those types never could keep things up.

From here, he could see the sign over the grill. CHEESEBURGER $2.50. And, right next to it, MEE KROB $1.39.

His mouth twisted in disgust. Mee krob. What the heck is that? He'd come here as a boy, after fishing with his father. Back then, you could get a plate of eggs and grits for less than a dollar. And there sure wasn't anything called mee krud on the menu.

He chuckled at his own joke. He sang along

with the radio. It wasn't easy to walk like a man in times like these.

That's why he had to mark out the path. And inspire others to follow. For a minute, he imagined the place gone. Leveled. Bodies flying through the air, smoke rolling like a great wave during a storm surge. A wave that picked up all the debris in its way. Washing the beach clean.

This would be his own personal project, he decided. The place he'd come as a boy. Back when everyone drove American cars, and diners just served burgers and coffee.

He'd see the place leveled. And then, in his memory, it would always be as he remembered it: clean, American.

He'd find the right time. But first, there was so much else to do. . . .

you've got mail!

To: whoever@cyberspace.com
From:randl.K
Subject:my severely rad adventures

It all started one night when I was totally bored.

Wait. I lied. Actually, it really started when Dad decided I was a total feeb. As in feeble-minded, for any postadolescents in the audience. Not that Dad used the word "feeb"—I think he said I was "in danger of losing brain cells from lack of use."

Says Dad: "All I hear you talk about is surfing and skateboarding. You're fifteen and a half years old, and you've moved on from toys to . . . toys."

So I made the mistake of saying: "Hey, Pop, at least I'm in step with my peers. And speaking of toys, did you notice that Beamer in the garage? I'm not holding the keys to that baby. I wish."

Which was a slight dig to Dad. I'm only two months away from getting my driver's license and Dad has informed me there is no way I'll be sliding behind the wheel of his BMW. He says I haven't shown the "correct level of maturity." Okay, we happened to be at the breakfast table at the time, and I happened to be balancing a spoon on the end of my nose. But, still.

Maybe he's a little touchy because the one time he did let me drive it around the mall parking lot, on a Sunday, mind you, I stalled out five times. The last time was right in front of a delivery truck. The truck driver had to jam on the brakes and came about a millimeter away from creaming the back bumper.

Anyway, back to Dad's dissatisfaction with my intellectual development. The next thing I know, MTV is slashed and burned for the duration. Then I have my very own subscription to the newspaper, and my dad-turned-Fascist-leader gives me a pop quiz on the headlines. Every morning.

Then one night Dad comes home with this state-of-the-art laptop computer for homework purposes. Every computer geek at school practically drools all over it. Thanks, Dad.

The trouble started when I broke it. It wasn't my fault! Yes, I spilled the Coke on it. But who could have foreseen the resulting major keyboard gunk buildup? I didn't want my dad to find out, so I took it to this hacker I know, Maya Bessamer. She's a girl, but she's a total cyberhead. She said she could fix it, no sweat. Then she charged me an arm and a leg. When I told her that the fact she charged me so much gave me a severely intense pain, she just gave me a real nasty look and said, "Live with it, dude."

Anyway, on my next trip to cyberspace, something happened. I got taken to a place I'd never been. And since I'm a curious kind of guy, I hung out. And that, friends, was my first mistake.

Don't worry. I made plenty more. Then I had to get real smart, real fast. That should have made Dad happy.

If only I didn't have to borrow the Beamer. . . .

1 / / knock-knox

The rain started Tuesday morning. By Wednesday, I was considering donating my brain to any scientist studying the effect of boredom on a teenage boy. By Thursday night, I was ready to jump out my bedroom window. But it's on the first floor, and I'd have landed about knee-deep in mud, so I reconsidered.

The weather guy on the news, the lame-o who shoots a water pistol at the weather map whenever it rains, said there was this tropical depression stalled out in the Atlantic Ocean somewhere.

Which meant no swimming. No skateboarding. What else was there to do in a beach town in Florida? Especially since my parents were on this "no TV except for PBS" kick.

And you think the *tropics* are depressed.

There was nothing left to do that night but bond with my laptop. When you can't surf the waves, surf the Internet. I hadn't logged on since Maya Bessamer had overhauled my computer.

I clicked on my "favorite places" icon. Then I waited to be zoomed down the information highway to my favorite webzine.

But I never got there. My computer had its own idea, and took a wrong turn somewhere. I found myself in a chat room. My online name got posted: randl.K. There were only ten other people chatting, but I decided to lurk for a few minutes and see if there was anything cool going on.

I have to admit, though, that in my humble opinion (or IMHO, in cybertalk), chat rooms are total snores. Somebody writes something like *Speed metal Rules!* and other people write *No way* and *You suck* and *Rap rules, you lame jerk* and you think you're going to go out of your stark-raving mind.

Lately, however, my best friend, Bemus, had been telling me that he's met all sorts of cool girls online. Lucky for Bemus, because if he had to talk to a girl face-to-face he'd probably hurl onto his high-tops.

I saw that someone named SwampFox was in the chat room, so I decided to stick. With a name like that, it could have been either a hot babe or a wacko who lived in the boonies. That's what's so cool about the Internet. You gets your modem, and you takes your chances.

But if there were any cool minds online in this group, they must have been snoozing. SwampFox couldn't get a word in edgewise. This dude PAT.riot73 was dominating the conversation, talking about how there were no "five-and-tens" on Main Street anymore. And there was just a bunch of Chinese restaurants. Every so often JamminGuy would chime in, saying *I hear you* or *were on the same page*. He sounded like a complete idiot.

This was bypassing Snoresville and heading straight for Coma Land.

But just as I got ready to click out, SwampFox asked me who I was.

randlK—stats?

Which meant, how old was I and was I a guy or a girl? Maybe I could get something started.

I typed in:

19/m. You?

Which isn't strictly true. Well, it's about four years away from being true. I'm not nineteen, I'm fifteen and a half. But as I may have mentioned, you can be whoever you want on the Internet. Besides, I'm incredibly mature. And I didn't want her to blow me off right away.

She wrote:

wow de wow. 19/f.

Things were finally getting interesting here. I tried to think of something clever to write, but PAT.riot73 cut in.

randlK, does your town have a Main Street?

Not really, I wrote. *We have strip malls. Florida is very big on malls.*

Then PAT.riot73 wrote that the group was made up of amateur city-planning fanatics.

Whoa. Lucky me.

Were into zoning, JamminGuy said. *It rules.*

zzzzzzz, right? SwampFox wrote, and I laughed.

LOL, I wrote, which means "laugh out loud" in computer-speak. *It doesn't exactly float my boat.*

But it controls your life, 60.MAN wrote. *You just don't know it.*

Somebody named OffRoad66 chimed in. *It's all about what goes where. Why. Who controls things.*

And the loudmouth PAT.riot73 wrote: *For instance, a business shouldn't be allowed to open right next to your house.*

Like a gas station, 60.MAN wrote.

Or a motel. Esp. an Indian one, SwampFox wrote. *You'd be smelling curry in your sleep!!*

But then PAT.riot73 cut her right off. *SwampFox, you're on my list for that. Rude.*

randl.K, what's the economy look like in your town?

I checked my watch. Bo-ring! Now we were talking about the help wanted ads?

Pretty standard, I wrote. *Tourism, stores.*

What did I know about my town's economy?

Any factories? OffRoad66 wrote.

Just the fish-processing place, I wrote. *And you don't want to get downwind of that. I work at the auto racetrack.*

I stared at the words on the screen. I didn't know why I wrote that. Probably because I was bored. And I wanted to impress SwampFox.

Cool. That was from OffRoad66.

!!!!!!!! from JamminGuy.

What do you do? PAT.riot73 wrote.

I thought it would be way too bold to say I raced cars. So I typed in: *Mechanic.*

Because that, in my opinion, would be a stoking profession. And it beat saying that I was a sophomore in high school and wasn't allowed to even *touch* the key of my dad's car.

You in the pit crew? OffRoad66 wrote.

You betcha.

!!!!!!!! JamminGuy wrote. Did he only have one key on his keyboard?

Where was SwampFox? She hadn't said much in a while. Maybe she was annoyed at

PAT.riot73 for telling her to shut up. I thought
about asking her if she wanted to go into a private room. But maybe it was too soon in our
relationship.

PAT.riot73 started talking again, and I lost
the chance.

*Time to tend to my business now. Remember
that the pride of your power can strengthen you.*

So now PAT.riot73 was turning into a self-
help guru?

What about the number? JamminGuy wrote.

Already gave it out, PAT.riot73 wrote back.
You don't want all of your friends calling.

But I didnt get it!!!!!

Wow, JamminGuy was proving that one
could whine in cyberspace.

Wait, I have a joke, SwampFox wrote.

knock knox
who's there?
tie-dye
tie-dye who?
tie-dye tonight—
saris tomorrow!

I didn't get the joke. So the girl had a lame
sense of humor. If she had long blond hair, I'd
overlook it.

Zip it!!!! PAT.riot73 wrote. *OK. 375 242-1030.*

I copied down the number, just for curiosity's sake. Why would JamminGuy be so whiny about a phone number? Maybe it was SwampFox's.

PAT.riot73 signed off. SwampFox said goodbye a second later, so I split.

What a bunch of weirdos. Except for SwampFox, of course. I pulled the phone toward me. Sure, I'd get blasted for making a long-distance call, but I was curious.

I dialed the number, and I got that lame recording: "Your call cannot be completed as dialed." I hung up. I didn't think my evening could possibly improve any further than listening to a bunch of lamebrains talk about zoning. So I went down to the kitchen and polished off the rest of the mocha-fudge ice cream from dessert.

2 // i read the news today, oh boy

The next morning, the Kincaid Family Kitchen was in full swing. It was the usual morning gig. Mom was drying her panty hose in the microwave while she wolfed down some whole-grain toast. Dad was ingesting tanks of coffee while he speed-read the paper. My seven-year-old sister, Rosie, sat dreamily chewing cereal. Her half-open mouth was crammed with soggy cornflakes. Not a pretty picture, let me tell you.

"Close your mouth, squirt, you're grossing me out," I said in a low voice as I passed her.

"Randy." Mom's voice was sharp as she whisked her panty hose out of the oven. She has ears like a wolf, my mom. "Be nice. It's too early."

But Rosie didn't care. She probably didn't even hear me. Don't ask me what the kid thought about. She was only seven, so it probably revolved around a doll or a princess. Rosie was the biggest girlie-girl in the world.

I poured an orange juice for me and an apple juice for Rosie, since I saw that my mom had forgotten. Mom was staring at the *Wall Street Journal* with a really intense expression on her face.

"Here's your paper, Randy," Dad said. He handed me my very own fresh copy of the *Bunnington Beach Beacon*.

"Thanks, Dad." I said this in my extra-manly voice. I called it my "Princeton" voice. I had to be careful, though. I didn't want him to think I was being sarcastic. Sarcasm does not go over well with parental figures.

The Princeton voice had a good effect on teachers, but Dad just rolled his eyes and asked me to pass the jam.

I buttered a bran muffin while I scanned the headlines. Rosie swirled a cornflake in her apple juice and ate it. What a gourmet.

What I couldn't understand was why adults read the paper, anyway. It was always the same. A war in some place you'd never heard of until there was a war there. A natural disaster in some place that had too many people crammed into too little space. Some politician saying some other politician wasn't worth dog drool. Throw in a city council meeting and boom, you got the front page.

But I flipped through the paper every morning for two reasons. Number one, it kept things copacetic with Pop. And B, after a minimum period spent on reading news, I felt free to flip to sports.

But today, a headline snagged my attention.

KNOXVILLE COMMUNITY CENTER JOINS BOMBING TOLL
No Injuries, but Building Destroyed

Lately, there'd been a string of bombings at community centers and recreation halls across the United States. The bombers always struck centers that provided services to immigrant populations. The FBI was pretty much tearing their hair out, but they had zero leads. They didn't even know if there was a conspiracy, or if the bombings were copycat crimes.

How do you like that? I actually *was* able to absorb facts from the morning paper. Chalk one up for Dad.

I read the first couple of paragraphs. It was pretty gruesome. Somebody had left an "incendiary device" in the day-care area. It was after hours, so nobody was hurt. But what kind of person would take that kind of risk?

A crazy wacko psycho, that's who.

I was just starting to move along to the sports

page when a sentence jumped out at me.

The Knoxville center was noted for its out-reach program to the fast-growing Thai popula-tion. . . .

It was just one of those weird tricks your mind plays on you. Because the words "Knoxville" and "Thai" started to play Ping-Pong in my brain. *Knock-knox . . .*

Why had SwampFox spelled "knock" that way? I thought it had been one of those cyber-spellings. If you spent much time in chat rooms, you knew that on the Net, spelling was a cre-ative subject.

Tie-dye tonight.

The next thing I knew, I was playing the "sounds like" game.

Thai die tonight.

An icy finger walked up my spine. I shivered. Too weird. My imagination was racing ahead of reality. Not an unusual occurrence, mind you.

I started to ease the sports section out from the rest of the paper.

"Anything good in the paper, Randy?" Dad asked. He took a look at his watch, so I relaxed. No quiz this morning. Dad was running late.

"Tons of interesting stuff," I said.

Just then, I noticed how my thumb had com-pletely smashed a raisin from my bran muffin on the front page. It looked like this really big mole on the chin of Mrs. Zonderway, the assistant principal.

That reminded me that if I was late for school one more time this month, I'd get detention. It was time to hustle.

Who says you never learn anything useful from the paper?

I hopped on my bicycle and zoomed to school. The storm front had moved on, and we were back from the Twilight Zone and in sunny Florida once again. Sunlight sparkled on the puddles. It was going to be a severely stellar day.

I pedaled fast down the streets, underneath the blue sky and the waving palm trees. I could smell the salty ocean, and the wind tickled my ears. As I got closer to Bunnington Beach High, I entered the Kid River. Guys and girls swarmed around me like salmon heading upstream. The freshmen were traveling in clumps toward school, the seniors were beeping the horns of their convertible Miatas to make sure everyone checked out their cool cars. The hoods were grinding out their cigarettes, the jocks were jostling elbows and bellowing "All-*right!*" like the idiots they were. The nerds were swinging backpacks over their shoulders and hitting other people in the head.

But they all had one thing in common. After all that rain, everyone looked relieved and almost happy, even if they were just going to school. No wonder a knock-knock joke had sent a shudder down my spine. Whose imagination wouldn't short out after three days of parental surveillance and constant exposure to a seven-year-old nutcake?

"It was the rain that did it," I said out loud as I locked my bike.

"Did what?" Maya Bessamer spoke up beside me. She was bending over to lock her bike, and I hadn't seen her. She's about the size of a four-year-old. Her brown eyes gleamed behind her platinum wire-rimmed glasses. "Turned you into a frog?"

"Whoa, hardy har," I said. "A facetious remark from Straight-A Bessamer. Should I alert the media?"

Maya pushed her glasses up her nose. "Definitely. You just used the word 'facetious' in a sentence. Wait—I can see the headline now. 'Surfer Dude Breaks the Two-Syllable Barrier.'"

Smirking, Maya slipped past me and walked away. Just when I was thinking of a really good zinger, too.

Save me from ninety-pound cybergeeks, will you? That girl was too etiquette-challenged to converse with. She was half-Vietnamese, and about the same size as Rosie. I could probably pick her up with one hand. Then I'd bring her right up to eye-level and say something really cutting, like, "Put a cork in it, half-pint!"

I sighed as I locked my bike. The problem was that Maya Bessamer was way smart. You couldn't cut her down to size. Even if she was only five feet tall.

"Whoa, dude." Bemus slouched up to me. "What are you doing trolling in the geek pond?" He jerked his head toward Maya, who was walking up the stairs to school.

"Just making pleasant conversation," I said. "She's in my driver's ed class."

"You're not thinking of asking Bessamer out, are you, dude?" Bemus asked.

"Of course not," I said. "Do you think I have a death wish?"

"Cool," Bemus said. "Because she is, like, a severious social goose egg." He made a circle of his thumb and forefinger and looked at me through it.

I was starting to admit to myself that sometimes Bemus got on my nerves. You wouldn't exactly call him Swifty, if you know what I mean.

It seriously bothered me that sometimes people got us confused. We were both skateboard wizards, and we kind of looked alike, I guess. We had the same asymmetrical haircut, and our hair was the same shade of sunstreaked blond. But my eyes were green, and his were brown. And I wore green high-tops, and he wore black.

Totally different.

"Like you're JFK, Jr.," I said.

Bemus snorted. "He wishes."

"No," I said. "You do."

"Do not."

What can I say? At Bunnington Beach High, the wit just flows.

After school, I rode home to switch to my skateboard and then hit the concrete with Bemus. There was a rad ramp near the interstate and we were working on perfecting our frontside nose grinds.

When it started to get dark, I scooted home. Mom and Dad both had to work late, so nobody could cook dinner. We had pizza delivered.

It is so way cool when life suddenly turns stellar after a downturn.

I almost didn't turn on my laptop that night. But it was either that or tackle my social studies homework. So I clicked on the icon and found myself in the chat room again.

This time, PAT.riot73 greeted me right away. SwampFox welcomed me back. They were having a talk about politics, they said. What did I think about taxes?

Whoa, too high, I wrote. *My paycheck seems to get smaller every week.*

What else could I say? I'd told them that I was a race car mechanic. And adults complained about their shrinking paychecks all the time.

The gang went on to talk about taxes. What is it with this group? Were they trying to zoom off the snoresville scale entirely? Once in a while I'd make a comment, just to let them know I was listening. No matter what boring thing PAT.riot73 said, I'd shoot in an *All right!* or a *Tell me about it.* Or I'd follow JamminGuy's lead and just write: *!!!!!!!*

Meanwhile, I kind of read my social studies assignment. I kept checking back to see if SwampFox would make another joke, or JamminGuy would say something really stupid. JamminGuy seldom disappointed me.

Then suddenly, I was in the spotlight. PAT.riot73 started asking me about my job. Whoops. Unlike the average teenage guy, I didn't know that much about cars. Just about stalling out a "thirty-five-thousand-dollar masterpiece of German engineering." That's a quote from Guess Who.

PAT.riot73 asked me how much horsepower was in a race car. Like I knew.

More than the average Dodge, I wrote.

Tell me. Do they use regular gas?

How should I know?

You have to add some major octane to get those babies moving, I wrote. *And then it's Blur City.*

High octane. Sounds fast. Wish I could pump some in my old tank, PAT.riot73 wrote.

Then JamminGuy jumped in.

Remember The Dukes of Hazzard? *That show ruled!*

Which seemed to tick off PAT.riot73.

It was slop, he wrote. *Why don't you try picking up a book, JamminGuy? It's a rectangular item with a cover, in case you've never seen one.*

I expected JamminGuy to come back with something cutting like *Go suck a pig's nose, PATriot!* but he just got quiet.

Okay, time to misplace my glasses, PAT.riot73 wrote. *And make some salt-water tea.*

Saltwater tea? PAT.riot73 had me there. It

sounded seriously gross to me. Why would somebody make tea out of salt water? Even my mom, who's seriously into health food, wouldn't go that far.

But "salt-water tea" sounded familiar, too. As if I'd seen it somewhere before. Maybe in the health food store my mom dragged me into while she bought adzuki beans.

If you want to know more about it, try 592 848-2355.

I scrawled down the number on the same paper I'd used to write down the number from last night. After everybody signed off, I called it. Not in service again. PAT.riot73 was not only a cranky bore, he couldn't figure out a simple phone number.

I surfed the Net for a while and listened in on a few more chat rooms. One of them was talking about alien abductions. Another group was discussing how Kool-Aid was part of a plot to make everyone radioactive.

That's when I decided these guys were just another example of the great truth—cyberspace was full of goofballs. I had just checked into one particular room of the Wacko Motel.

It was time for a dose of reality. So I sneaked downstairs and switched on MTV.

3//worst-case scenario

I guessed I overdid it on the music videos, because I stayed up too late, and the next morning my eyes felt sandy, like I'd fallen asleep during a windstorm at the beach. In the kitchen, I passed up my usual cheery "Greetings, Earthlings," and grunted hello to the clan instead.

So my brain was still snoozing when I reached for the paper. It took a bunch of concentration to make sense of the headline. And you know that concentration is not my best feature.

SECOND BOMBING IN TWO DAYS: MISSISSIPPI TOWN HIT
Two Children Killed

I blinked, trying to focus. It was the picture that grabbed my eye. A woman sat on a curb. Behind her, the charred remains of a building still smoked. You couldn't see the woman's face because it was buried in her hands. She wore a long dress.

The town was called Godette. The victims were immigrants from India.

I kept staring at the paper, waiting for it to make sense. Something tickled at the back of my brain. I kept reading.

The FBI had been called in. There were similarities to the other hate crimes. . . . No leads, though the authorities suspected a conspiracy network spread over at least several states. . . . Coming on the heels of the bombing in Knoxville, the South was held in a grip of fear. . . .

Conspiracy network.

Knock-knox . . .

Tie dye tonight. Saris tomorrow . . .

Saris. Those dresses Indian women wore.

Whoa. Time to chill. I took a sip of my juice and looked around the bright kitchen. Everything looked so normal. So normal that there seemed to be no way I could be thinking what I was thinking. Actually, I wasn't sure exactly *what* I was thinking. But I had to be wrong.

I looked at the photo of the woman, her face buried in her hands. I could imagine how her shoulders shook as she cried. Now, behind her, I could make out a small body on a stretcher.

Like those Indian motels. . . . You'd be smelling curry in your sleep. . . .

The coincidences had gone from weird to downright scary. Why would SwampFox mention tie dye and then saris, one after the other, as if she was *predicting* what was going to happen?

Could I have stumbled onto the conspiracy group that was bombing community centers? Could those geeks chatting about zoning actually be *killers*?

A crumb from my bran muffin stopped halfway down my throat. I started to cough, and I couldn't stop. Mom ran over and patted my back. My dad was poised to give me the Heimlich maneuver, so I quickly reached for my orange juice. That helped.

"Are you all right, Randy?" Mom asked me, her face worried.

I took another sip of juice. "Fine," I croaked. "Just had trouble swallowing something."

Mom and Dad went back to scarfing down breakfast. Rosie blew into the milk in her cereal bowl, trying to make a tidal wave.

I looked back at the paper. You bet I had trouble swallowing this. Because it was crazy. There just wasn't any connection.

No way.

It was just a coincidence. *But what if it was true?*

I looked at my Dad over the newspaper. I

didn't have to say a word. I could fast-forward and see an instant Coming Attraction of David Kincaid's Opinion of His Son, Part Deux.

You think you've uncovered a terrorist conspiracy on the Internet? No more TV or movies until you're thirty, young man.

Look, I'll be the first to admit it. I'm not a straight-A student. Nowhere near. Everybody thinks my biggest challenge is choosing which stencil to put on my skateboard.

And, yeah, my imagination gets me in trouble sometimes. No question.

But kids had been killed.

What if the worst-case scenario were true? What if I was, gulp, *right*?

Mom always says that she doesn't know where her two kids got their imaginations. She and Dad are both in business. Dad is president of marketing for this company that makes wrapping paper and greeting cards. Mom manages an office for this huge firm that does something or other. I can never remember.

Not exactly artistic types.

Meanwhile, their kids are total opposites. Take Rosie. For two whole years, she pretended to be Dorothy from *The Wizard of Oz* and that she and the Tin Man were married. For a whole month last year, I had to call her "Mrs. Tin Man." No, I'm not making it up.

As for *moi,* my brain doesn't seem to work in that straight road, No Turns, No Outlet kind of way. Think of one of those triangular yellow signs with the wavy arrow that means Curves Ahead. That's how I imagine the inside of my bean.

For example, speaking of road signs, when I was eight, we went to Yosemite. There were these signs all over saying WATCH OUT FOR FALLING ROCKS. I decided that Falling Rocks was some guy who murdered campers in their sleeping bags. I actually convinced myself that this was true. I didn't sleep a wink.

So I was probably way off base with this bombing thing. But the more I tried *not* to think about it, the more I did. At school, I was even spacier than usual, which means I gave the impression of someone inhabiting Venus.

Finally, at lunch, I took my sandwich out to the bleachers and stopped fighting the urge. I let my imagination go.

Say there *was* a conspiracy group who met on the Internet. And say this group *did* have something to do with the bombings. What next?

While I chowed down on my tuna, I thought back over the conversation in the chat room. Sure, it was dull. But maybe it was *deliberately* dull. Maybe as soon as a stranger signed on, they downshifted into safe topics to scope the person out. If the person got bored and signed off, that was okay, too. Less dangerous.

But maybe even while they were chatting, they were still giving clues to each other. That seemed like something a conspiracy group would do. So even though it seemed like they were talking about normal stuff, there were clues if you knew what to look for. The topics were kind of weird for chat groups—most groups talked about movies, or things they had in common, like fly-fishing or being abducted by aliens. These guys talked about five-and-dime stores, zoning rules, taxes . . . what freaks would *want* to talk about that stuff, besides politicians?

I finished my tuna, then polished off an apple and an oatmeal cookie. And I still hadn't come up with any bright ideas.

I stood at my locker, hauling out the volume the size of the Miami phone directory that was better known as my social studies textbook. Behind me, I heard a bunch of kids talking about "the big game."

There's always a "big game" in high school.

One of the girls said in a squeaky voice that she needed a ride. I sneaked a look over my shoulder to scope out a total bombshell who was way out of my league. The bombshell told the squeaker that she'd pick her up with the others.

"Call me and I'll tell you what time," Bombshell said, flicking a strand of white-blond hair behind her shoulder.

"But I don't have your number!" the squeaker said.

Bombshell took Squeaker's hand and started writing on it with her pen. It was a totally Cool Crowd thing to do. Squeaker would probably break a leg getting to a piece of paper to write the number down before it smeared.

"555–23— is that a 7 or a 2?" Squeaker asked Bombshell.

But I didn't hear Bombshell's reply. My hand froze on the combination lock of my locker. I heard numbers in the air behind me. I saw numbers dance on the lock in front of me.

Numbers!

The phone number! For two nights in a row, PAT.riot73 had given it out. And I'd called it. Both times, the number just didn't make sense.

It was like a Roman candle shot off in my brain. Maybe the number *did* make sense. To someone who knew the key. Maybe the number was the code!

4//spy stuff

I had a few minutes before class, so I ran to the library, where was a phone book. I looked up the area codes of both numbers. Bingo! The first three numbers didn't correspond with an area code in the United States.

The bell rang, so I made tracks to my geometry class. While Mr. Nash droned on about trapezoids, I tried to remember everything I knew about codes.

I had read a book once on famous spy cases. It was a long time ago, back when I still read books. But I remembered some stuff.

Codes were simple, in a way. You just assigned a different meaning to the letters or numbers than you saw. To break the code, you either had to get hold of the code book the other guys were using, or try all sorts of different combinations to figure out the system. I had a feeling that if JamminGuy could understand whatever code this group was using, it couldn't be too difficult.

But then again, a simple trapezoid could severely strain my brain.

After school, I sat in my room with a piece of paper and wrote down the cities where the bombings took place and the numbers that PAT.riot73 had given out.

KNOXVILLE, TENNESSEE
375 242-1030
GODETTE, MISSISSIPPI
592 848-2355.

Maybe the numbers told the group which city was going to be hit next. PAT.riot73 was the mastermind. He was the one who always gave out the numbers. And, once I thought about it, I realized that it always happened around 7:45 P.M.

First I tried taking the letters of the alphabet and giving them corresponding numbers. A=1, B=2, and so on, but that gave me nothing. Besides, it was way too easy.

Maybe there was another key. Maybe something in the conversation would help me.

I listened in that night, then every night for almost a week. All PAT.riot73 did was blab about taxes and the "home of the brave" and give lessons on the American Revolution.

JamminGuy kept saying *U R Right on!*

And *!!!!!!!*

SOS—Same Old Stuff. No clues.

So maybe there was a code book. A book they all had, so they could look up whatever number PAT.riot73 gave out. When they first started the group, PAT.riot73 could have made up his own code book and e-mailed it to them. Or even used snail mail. In that case, I was sunk.

But having so many obvious code books floating around could be dangerous. Usually, code books were something that every spy had, so it wouldn't look suspicious. Like the Bible. Or a phone book. One case I read about used a bird-watching book.

There were probably about a gadzillion possibilities. I just had to wait and hope I got a clue online.

I carried that paper around in my pocket for over a week. A couple of times a day I took it out and just stared at it. I felt pretty stupid, because nothing new occurred to me.

Every morning, I raced down for the paper. If I really was on the right track, I didn't think there would be another bombing, since PAT.riot73 hadn't given out another number. But I still had to check.

My dad was totally impressed with my new dedication to current events.

"Glad to see you're taking an interest in the news," he said. "I told you you'd get hooked."

"Right, Dad," I said in my Princeton voice. He even relaxed the TV rule and let me watch it for an hour after supper. But I told him I'd rather go online.

Now Dad thought he was a genius for improving his son's intellectual pursuits. I'm tell-ing you. I should get a medal.

History makes me zone. What can I say? When you look around my neighborhood, you don't tend to connect with anything older than, say, 1960. I used to be sort of interested in that kind of stuff when I was kid. I used to read books about Patrick Henry, or was it Davy Crockett? But who cares what happened to some bozo back in 1776?

Or, actually, 1773. Which was when the Boston Tea Party happened. Which was what my oh-so-spellbinding social studies teacher, Mr. Pogue, was explaining. Which was why my eyes were closing and my head kept jerking as I'd catch myself falling asleep. Jessica Manderly, the coolest girl in my class, kept snickering at me, but I couldn't stay awake. That's how boring Mr. Pogue was. I was risking the contempt of a serious babe with long blond hair.

Let me tell you about Mr. Pogue. I had him for driver's ed, too, and I swear he could induce a coma with his lecture on parallel parking. He was one of those teachers who made jokes that aren't funny, trying to get on your good side. He was always winking at students and saying, "I'm not ancient, you know. I still remember my high school days, heh heh."

But here's the sad thing—nobody liked him. Nobody called him Poguey or The Poguemeister. Nobody joked with him after class, the way they did with Mr. Adams, the biology teacher, or red-headed Madame Bernstein, the head of the French Club.

Maybe because as soon as he opened his mouth, you nodded off.

"Tea party . . . ," I heard as I slipped into dreamland. *Long blond hair . . .*

1773 . . . Jessica on my skateboard . . . Redcoats . . . Jessica in a red coat . . . Patriots . . .

I jerked awake. Jessica snickered, and I pretended that I was doing the old arm and finger stretch.

Patriot 73!

It fit. The guy was an American Revolution

fanatic. But after exercising the old bean on this piece of information, I couldn't figure out any way it could hold a key to the code.

Mr. Pogue started jawing about the Intolerable Acts. I thought about informing him that his teaching style was intolerable, but I didn't think he'd find it amusing, somehow.

Instead, I settled in for another nap.

Tea . . . colonists . . . Boston Harbor . . . don't tread on me . . . snakes . . . snakes drinking tea . . . salt-water tea . . .

My head jerked up again so fast, it hit Dobie Cairns, who was also napping during Mr. Pogue's class. Jessica Manderly burst out laughing.

But I didn't even care.

I figured out the code book! And here was the funniest part of the whole thing.

I'd had the book all along.

5//salt-water tea

Saltwater tea had done it. Suddenly, the misty seas of my ancestral memory had parted, and I'd remembered way far back in my life. Back when I'd read books.

I had loved this book, *Johnny Tremain,* when I was a kid. I'd read it about twelve thousand times. "Salt-water Tea" was the title of a chapter in it. The chapter was about how this kid Johnny takes part in the Boston Tea Party, when the patriots wore disguises and boarded these ships. They threw all the British tea in the harbor.

Salt-water tea—get it?

Ka-ching!

I blew off Bemus after school. He wanted to head to the beach, and he looked at me as though I was totally insane when I said I had homework.

The wheels of my bike were smoking as I hauled my posterior section back home. I pounded up the stairs to my room and went on a major search for my old copy of *Johnny Tremain*. It wasn't in my bookshelf, but there was a box of books in my closet Mom was saving for Rosie.

I practically tore the box apart. *Johnny Tremain* was at the very bottom, of course. It's a rule of life, in my opinion, that when you're looking for something, it's always at the bottom of the box or on the back of the shelf. Am I right?

I flipped through the hardcover book quickly. "Salt-water Tea" was the sixth chapter.

Now what?

Then I saw the title of another chapter called "The Pride of Your Power." Wasn't that what PAT.riot73 had said that first night? I remembered thinking he sounded like some infomercial guru on TV. Then, that very night, the center in Knoxville burned down.

I spread out the paper that I'd copied the phone numbers on. Then I flipped to the chapter called "Salt-water Tea." If I was right, all I had to do was count the letters from the beginning of the chapter. Each number would correspond to a letter. And the letters should spell out at least part of the word "Godette," the town in Mississippi.

The first number was 5. And it should correspond to a "G." I counted in five letters, but I got an "N." Then I tried counting down five lines, but I got a different letter again.

So maybe this wasn't going to be so easy.

I'm going to do you a big favor here. I'm going to skip the part where I sat there like a dolt and wrote down letters and crossed them out. I'm leaving out the part where I shook the book like a chimpanzee. Ditto when I threw it across the room.

Because this code was not diggable. In other words, it didn't make sense. I couldn't figure it out. Maybe my secret suspicion about myself was true: I was stupid. Could it be that my dad could be, gasp, *right* after all?

I stared at the letters and words so long that they started to do the mambo.

Then, suddenly, I had an idea.

All the other letters were pretty common. But the "X" in Knoxville wasn't. My dad is a Scrabble fiend, and we play sometimes. I knew that "X" was worth about a billion points because it was rare to find a word that contained an "X."

So maybe I should work *backward*.

I turned to "The Pride of Your Power" chapter.

Since "X" is the fourth letter in "Knoxville," maybe the fourth number in the series referred to "X": 2.

But there was no "X" in the second word. Or the second line.

So I read until I found the first "X." It was the thirtieth letter in the twelfth line.

Which didn't help me a bit.

I was back to square one.

When I woke up the next morning, my cheek was pressed into the binding of *Johnny Tremain*. There was this really big red welt on the side of my face. I looked like I'd been tortured by some sick librarian.

I rubbed the welt, as though that would make it disappear.

That's when it hit me. The evidence was staring me in the face.

I had a *hardcover* copy of *Johnny Tremain*. An *old* hardcover copy.

Johnny Tremain had to be out in paperback.

The book was some sort of classic, so they probably kept it in print all the time.

The chat room group couldn't be using the same edition as I was! No wonder I couldn't crack the code!

I got dressed at warp speed. I scarfed down a banana and a muffin and scanned the paper so my dad wouldn't go on his usual Randy Rag. Then I hopped on my bike.

I pedaled down the block toward school, just in case my mom was watching from the window. Sometimes she likes to check out whether I'm riding like a maniac or not. At the corner I made a right, then circled back on the next block and headed downtown.

The bookstore was closed. It was only eight-thirty. They opened in an hour. I should have figured that, but I'd been too excited. Now, I could have either hauled my posterior over to school and made my first class, or I could have waited. If I skipped my morning classes, it would have been huge trouble. I could have just come back to the bookstore after school. That would have been the smart thing to do.

But since when does Randy Kincaid do the smart thing? Just ask my dad.

So I waited.

I parked my bike by a tree. Then I parked myself on a bench by a bus stop. All the commuters gave me the hairy eyeball for taking up valuable bench space, but I zoned them out.

After about twenty minutes, I went and got a

yogurt shake, just to have something to do.

The minutes crawled by. Finally, I saw this skinny guy head to the front door of the bookstore. He took out a bunch of keys.

I shot to my feet and dashed over. He looked over his shoulder at me.

"I don't carry CD-ROMs."

"I'm looking for a book," I said.

"What do you know. A teenage boy who reads." He unlocked the door and swung it open. "Catch me when I faint."

What was this, the Comedy Bookstore?

I hurried into the store. The skinny guy turned on the lights. He went straight to the coffee machine.

"The new R. L. Stine isn't in yet," he said over his shoulder.

"I'm not looking for *Goosebumps*," I said.

"Be still my heart," the guy said, shaking coffee into a filter. "Young adult section is at the back."

I hurried down the crowded aisle. *Johnny Tremain* was written by Esther Forbes. I found a paperback copy right away. It was new, and much cheaper than the hardcover. I could even picture JamminGuy springing for it.

I plunked my money down on the counter. Mr. Comedian Bookseller picked up *Johnny Tremain*.

"Don't tell me. You have to get this for school, right?"

I shook my head. "I already read it. I want to read it again."

"Sonny, you've made my day." He put the book in a bag, and fished around for change. My nerves were screaming, at this point. I beat out a drum solo on the counter.

He handed me the bag and the change. I took off, fast.

"You must really love this book!" he called after me.

The bell jangled, and the door *whooshed* shut behind me. I ran back to the bench by the bus stop.

Traffic roared around me. Bus exhaust choked me. And I sat, counting lines and words.

I worked back from the "X." In this edition, it was the thirtieth letter on the tenth line.

I took out the paper with the numbers on it.
375 242-1030

And the numbers stared up at me: 1030.

That meant that each letter was represented by *two* numbers. The first referred to the *line*. The next referred to how many letters you had to count over.

I went back to the beginning of the number.

3 7. I counted down three lines. Counted over seven letters: **K**

It worked! I looked at the next two numbers:
5 2

I counted down five lines. Counted over two letters: **N**

Down four. Over two: **O**

The "1" obviously didn't refer to the first line. That meant that when a number was followed by a zero, you multiplied by ten.

So I counted down ten lines. Over thirty: **X**

I stared down at the piece of paper: **K N O X**

My heart thundered and my fingers trembled as I turned to the "Salt-water Tea" chapter. I counted down lines and letters and spelled out **G O D E T**

It was just enough letters to figure out the target. Somehow, PAT.riot73 must have also given the clue to the state. I still had to figure that part out.

I sat, staring down at the piece of paper.

I couldn't believe my own eyes. Could I really have figured it out?

But I knew that I had.

I had the key. I'd broken the code.

6//runaround randy

I didn't jump up and yodel, "All *right*!" I didn't shout, "Awesome!" I just kept sitting there, staring down at the paper in my lap.

Because all along, it had been a kind of game. No way could I have stumbled onto some sick conspiracy to firebomb community centers all over the United States. It just didn't make sense.

It was too much for me to handle.

I looked up and down the street. There had to be a policeman around somewhere. Or a police station. That's what I needed. Some calm, cool detective who would copy down everything I had to say, take it off my hands, and then thank me for saving civilization.

"So you figured out the code," the detective said.

"When I got the copy of *Johnny Tremain*," I said, nodding. "The paperback, though. You can't use the hardcover . . . aren't you going to write that down?"

"Sure, kid." The detective scribbled on a pad. He was a blond guy with very hairy arms and a sunburn on the back of his neck. Probably went fishing on his day off. "Tell me again why you're not in school today?"

"Teachers' meeting. All day," I said. "Do you understand about the code? When a 0 follows a number, it means to multiply by 10."

"Right."

"They haven't given out a new number, so I don't think they're planning any more bombings," I said. "Not yet. Do you have a computer expert here?"

"What do we look like, IBM?" the detective said.

"Look, somebody has to figure out what the address of the chat group is. I mean, it's an icon on my computer, so—"

"Right."

"Aren't you going to write *that* down?"

"Sure, kid." Detective Hairy Arms smiled at me. Why didn't I trust him?

A policeman walked up and handed the detective a piece of paper. He read it.

He looked over the desk at me. "Busted, kiddo."

Busted? Did he think *I* was the bomber?

Suddenly, I got a sick feeling in my stomach.

He waggled a thick finger at me. "You're playing hooky. And you're busting my chops. That sort of thing annoys me, kid. Should I call your parents? Or should I just call your principal?" He folded his arms and leaned back in his chair. "If you were me, what would you do?"

I had about a split second to think.

"I'd let me go to the bathroom," I blurted. "Especially if I knew that I really needed to go."

He sighed and stood up. "Follow me."

We started across the squad room. But suddenly, Detective Hairy Arms stopped. He lifted his head like a dog hearing a train in the distance. "Do I smell Krispy Kreme?" he bellowed.

"Dave just brought 'em in," another cop said, munching on a cruller.

Detective Hairy Arms practically drooled onto his shirt. I could see that he'd completely lost interest in his big case. When you stack a kid playing hooky against a glazed Bavarian cream, who's going to win?

"Don't move, kid," Detective H. A. warned over his shoulder as he headed for the corner of the squad room. Next to a full coffeepot sat a huge open box of glistening doughnuts.

I might not be the brightest bulb in the chandelier, but I'm not stupid.

I ran.

For my next attempt to inform the authorities, I played it safe. Instead of showing up in my baggy shorts and T-shirt trying to look serious, I did the smart thing. I phoned the local FBI office and left an anonymous tip.

This was not as easy as it sounds. I got transferred about ten times, and put on hold. The whole time I was afraid they might be tracing the call. It was pretty nerve-racking.

Finally, this Agent Vorshack got on the phone. I thought I was getting my point across, because she didn't interrupt. She just made M&M noises. Which means she went "mm mm" a lot, like she was really listening. Or maybe she was eating a doughnut, too.

"So," I said when I finished. "Did you get all that?"

There was a pause. "Tell me something, R. K.," she said. "How old are you?"

She didn't believe me, either. "Forget about it," I said, and hung up.

I didn't know what else to do, so I headed back to school. I got a late pass, but the assistant principal had already called my dad.

The verdict? Grounded.

I lay on my bed, the laptop by my side. PAT.riot73 wasn't talking much, which was unusual. JamminGuy was dominating the conversation.

He had decided that satellite dishes were secret eavesdropping devices.

It's a govt conspiricy!!!!! he wrote.

U think ever-thang is a govt consp! wrote SwampFox.

LOL, wrote OffRoad66.

I decided to grab old Bessie by the horns.

I wrote:

IMHO, there's a foreign conspiracy to take away our jobs. There aren't enough to go around!

"IMHO" means "in my humble opinion." Maybe I could provoke them into a discussion. And then they would start to trust me.

We are on the same pg!!!!!!! JamminGuy wrote. *And I M tired of playin possom. I want Action!!!!!*

It worked!

But then PAT.riot73 broke in.

My mama always taught me not to discuss politics and religion, esp. with strangers. What did your mama teach you, JamminGuy?

I waited, watching the screen. Nobody said anything for a while.

I'm not interested in politics anyways, JamminGuy finally wrote. *Their all crooks.*

So much for the ambush. Everybody started chatting about this new action-adventure movie.

I lurked on the chat line for another hour, but it was the usual eye-closing stuff, even duller than usual.

I was getting frustrated. I had to come up with something more concrete. Something that would show people that I was on the level.

But when I'd mentioned getting the icon off my hard drive, Detective H.A. had looked at me like I'd started speaking Tonganese or something. He'd been so sarcastic, too. "Who do we look like, IBM?"

Suddenly, I bolted upright again. Every hair on my arms seemed to stand at attention.

All at once I'd thought of the question that I should have asked at the very beginning. A question that could lead me to bust the whole group wide open, if I could find out the answer.

All along, I'd been trying to move forward. Listening every night, waiting for the next clue. But what I had to do was move *backward*. Just like I had when I'd figured out the code.

Because here was the million-dollar question: *How did that icon get on my hard drive in the first place?*

7//everybody knows a geek

Maya Bessamer was waiting by the driver's ed car, eating a green apple. She always arrived first for our driver's ed class. Probably because she didn't have anything better to do.

"What's up, Beavis?" she asked me coolly.

But I wasn't going to be baited this time. I wanted answers that only a geek could give me.

"I have a couple of questions for you," I said. "About my computer."

Maya took a bite of her apple. "You're on the clock, then."

"You're going to *charge* me?"

She shrugged, chewing. "Time is money."

"Dream on, Bessamer," I said. "You can't charge me. Number one, you cleaned me out last time. And B, you messed up. I've got a problem with my hard drive, thanks to you."

Maya waved her apple at me. "I sincerely doubt it. But go ahead. Just try not to ask me a dumb FAQ, will you? I've had a bad day."

"I'm sooooo sorry," I said. "Is there anything I can do?"

Maya made a face at me. Or maybe it was indigestion from that green apple.

"What's an FAQ, anyway?" I asked.

"A 'frequently asked question,' newbie," Maya said. She gave this totally overdone, weary sigh. "So what seems to be the problem?"

"What would happen, say, if you transferred something onto my hard drive?" I said. "Say it was something from someone else's computer? Like, some kind of shortcut that zooms you to, like, an address on the Internet?"

Maya scowled. "What's all this say I did this and like an address? Try to, like, speak English."

"Whatever, man. What I'm saying is, say it was, like, an address someone shouldn't go to, like some group that you should be—"

Maya tossed her apple core right past my ear. I actually felt the rush of wind as it went by. It sailed over the roof of the car and rattled into the trash can. Two points.

"Save it," she said. "Kincaid, the air is whistling through your ears so fast, I'm catching cold. You're not making any sense."

I drew myself up to my full height, which meant I towered over her completely. She wore black jeans and this little white T-shirt with an edging of lace around the neckline, and tiny silver earrings shaped like tiny bells hung from her tiny earlobes.

Everything about her was delicate. But, somehow, she came across like a two-ton tank.

"All I'm saying is—," I started.

"Here comes Josh," she said. "Save your concentration for your driving. You can use it."

There wasn't much I could say to that. Number one, I had made the mondo mistake of telling everybody the story of stalling the Beamer out five times in the mall parking lot and almost getting creamed by a truck that said Safety First. And B, last week in driver's ed I'd driven up on somebody's lawn by mistake. I'd caught a glimpse of the ocean and was trying to see if the surf was up.

Josh Fallows walked up, the last member of our crack driving team. He was the quiet loner type, but out of the three of us, he was the best driver. I hated that.

"Hey," Josh grunted. He is one of those guys who barely opens his mouth when he talks. I wasn't sure who his friends were. He isn't a jock and he isn't a hood. He isn't a speed metal freak, or even a nerd, exactly. Which means, in high school land, that he is a nobody.

"I wanted to say thanks for fixing my computer," Josh said to Maya.

"You've got a regular business going, Bessamer," I said. "Are you out to bankrupt the entire class?"

"LOL, Kincaid," Maya answered in a fake sweet voice. She turned back to Josh. "I know how I feel when I can't get online. Did all your chat buddies miss you?"

Josh shrugged. The tips of his ears were glowing red. "I dunno. I guess." He stared at Maya, then quickly looked down.

Whoa. What a whiz kid.

"But now you're cruising again," Maya said.

He nodded. "I'm jammin'."

I froze. Jammin'! And Maya had fixed his computer.

Sure, it was current slang. But what were the odds of someone using it like that? Someone whose computer Maya had worked on? And Josh had seemed awfully guilty when Maya had mentioned his favorite chat room.

It all added up. Maya must have accidentally transferred Josh's icon onto my computer.

I've said this before: The cool thing about being online is that you can be anybody you want. I've even heard of Internet rooms where you can pretend to be a dog.

It made sense. Josh is a loner. He doesn't have many friends. He is exactly the kind of guy who could get hooked into a conspiracy group. They wouldn't have to know how young he was. They wouldn't have to know anything about him.

When Mr. Pogue appeared at my elbow, I didn't see him. I was too busy trying to figure Josh out.

"Good afternoon, all," he said. "Ground control to Major Randy. Are you ready to decimate someone's lawn today?"

You see? That's why he wasn't popular. If Mr. Adams had said that, I would have laughed. But there was something kind of mean in the way Mr. Pogue said it.

"Let's get started," Maya said. "Can I go first today?"

"Pushy, pushy," Mr. Pogue said. He tried to sound like he was teasing, but Maya blushed. Now we both hated him.

"I want Josh to start today," Mr. Pogue said.

"That's okay," Josh mumbled. "Maya can go first."

Mr. Pogue unlocked the car. "No, Josh. There's a lot of traffic around school. When we get to the empty roads, Maya can drive."

Mr. Pogue got in the front seat on the passenger side. "Let's head 'em up and move 'em out!" he called.

Josh hesitated. He looked at Maya, then looked away. Then he stomped toward the car.

I got into the backseat with Maya. Josh's eyes were on her in the rearview mirror. Then Mr. Pogue told him to get the lead out, and he jammed on the gas.

Why was Josh staring at Maya? She definitely looked part Asian. Maybe he resented her for that. Maybe he hated her.

Josh Fallows was looking mighty suspicious. I was going to keep my eye on him.

I brooded about Josh through the whole lesson, which probably wasn't too smart. I made some really stupid moves, like going through a stop sign and hitting a no parking sign while I was trying to parallel park.

It wasn't my fault. I couldn't concentrate. I was trying to think of a question that would trip up Josh, if he were JamminGuy.

Have you ever read Johnny Tremain?

Answer yes or no to this statement: Do you think satellite dishes are reprogramming your brain?

Hypothetically, would you ever get involved in an underground hate group that blows up community centers?

Finally, class was over. Maya was the last

driver, and she pulled back into the school parking lot.

Mr. Pogue wiped his forehead with a handkerchief. I guess I'd put him through the wringer. Then he said good-bye and hurried away.

Usually, I split the instant class was over. But today, I was trying to think of a way to trip up Josh. How could I do it without tipping him off?

"Well, see you guys," Maya said, and started across the parking lot.

Josh grunted a good-bye at me. He headed off in the opposite direction from Maya. I turned back toward school to pick up my skateboard.

I looked back once. To my surprise, I saw Josh jump over the bike rack, give a quick guilty look around, and then trot after Maya. I could tell he was trying to keep out of sight.

Quickly, I ran along the side of the building. I peeked around, just in time to see Maya cross the street and head down Willow. With another guilty look around, Josh sped after her.

He was following her!

So I found myself tailing Josh, who was tailing Maya. If you think that's easy, guess again. Once I had to dive into bushes on someone's front lawn, and I ripped my favorite T-shirt.

Finally, Maya stopped at this pink Spanish-style house with a big pile of rocks stacked in the front yard. She waved at a girl in overalls who was cutting orchid blossoms. The girl was older than Maya, maybe in her twenties, and had a long braid, almost down to her waist. She looked as if she could be Maya's sister, if it were possible for Bessamer to have a cute sibling.

I hid next to the garage at the house across the street. Maya and the girl started talking, and then they walked into the house.

Josh ducked behind a tree. He watched the house for a long time, as though he was casing the joint.

Then he reached into his backpack and took out a small brown bag.

I froze. *A bomb.*

I M tired of playin' possom, Jammin had wrote, misspelling a word, as usual. *I want Action!!!!!*

Josh looked around again. The street was quiet. I pressed up against the wall of the garage.

He darted across the street, sprinted across the lawn, and left the bag on the front steps. Then he knocked, leaped down the stairs, and bolted across the street again. He kept on running around the corner and disappeared.

Maya opened the door. She picked up the bag and started to open it—

"Noooooooo!" I yelled as I sprang out of my hiding place and ran toward her. I waved my arms frantically. "Don't touch it! Don't open it!"

Maya looked up, startled. I raced across the lawn and snatched the bag from her grasp. I threw it as hard as I could, across the lawn toward the street. The momentum of the throw made me lose my balance, and I fell off the steps onto the grass.

The bag turned in the air. It opened. A hail of chocolate chip cookies thunked to the earth. Then a plastic container fell and splattered something gooey onto the Bessamer front yard. A plastic fork dropped to the ground a second later.

I lay back on the grass, panting. I had a funny feeling that I'd just made a complete idiot of myself.

I'd thrown away someone's lunch.

Maya crossed over to where I lay. From down there on the grass, she looked almost . . . tall.

She peered down into my face with a look of contempt.

"What is the matter with you?" she said.

8//the x posse

I knew I had to be at my most severely eloquent
if I wanted to get out of the Bessamer front yard
in one piece. "I—uh—"

"Are you out of your *mind*?" Maya cut in.

Let me tell you something. It's hard to come
up with words in your own defense when you're
lying on your back and a pint-sized she-wolf is
standing over you.

I got to my feet. I tried my Princeton voice,
and I looked her right in the eye, the same way
I do when I'm snowing my dad. "Obviously, I
made a mistake."

"Obviously!" Maya stormed. "Why did you
throw that bag away?"

"Well." I thought about this. What reason
could I give, except the truth? "I thought it was
a bomb."

Maya's face flushed pink. "Who do you think
you're talking to, Kincaid? One of your airhead
buddies? You think I'm going to *buy* this?"

Maya stomped off and began to pick up the cookies and shove them into the bag.

"I'm serious!" I said. "I thought—"

"You thought Mrs. Fallows' shrimp salad and Josh's chocolate chip cookies were a bomb," Maya snapped. She picked up the plastic container and shoved it back in the bag. She wiped her hands on her jeans, then pushed her bangs off her forehead in an aggravated way. "Look, he uses too much baking soda, but they're not that bad."

"Why is Josh Fallows leaving food on your doorstep, anyway?" I asked hotly.

The flush on Maya's face went from delicate pink to bright red. "Because."

"Because why?"

"Because once we were talking before driver's ed about food we liked, and I said I liked shrimp salad, and he said his mom made the best. And I was polite and said, gee, I'd like to try it sometime. And then he told me that he bakes chocolate chip cookies, and I said they were my favorite kind of cookie."

"So *why* is he leaving that stuff on your stoop?" I asked. I still didn't get it.

"Because he has a crush on me, dodo," Maya snapped.

"Yeah, right," I hooted. Some dude had a

crush on Maya Bessamer? I didn't think so!

Maya's eyes narrowed. Perhaps I had made a tiny mistake.

She took a step toward me, and I stepped back. "Get off my lawn, Kincaid," she spit out. "I don't care why you're here. It's just some airhead, brainless, cotton candy, bleached-blond *plot* to make me crazy, right? And then you can tell all your airhead buddies about it!"

She put her two hands on my chest and pushed. And she was *strong*.

I stumbled back. "Hey! I resent that! I'm a natural blond!"

She turned her back. "Get lost."

But I didn't move. What was I doing? I had succeeded in alienating the one person who could help me. Without Maya Bessamer, I was nowhere.

"You know, I think maybe we're getting off on the wrong foot," I said.

Maya didn't turn. "I didn't hear anything. Because you are gone, Kincaid."

"Maya, I meant what I said before, in driver's ed," I said very fast before she went into the house. "I *do* need your help. *That's* why I did this. I really was trying to protect you from something. I wasn't trying to make fun of you."

"Tell it to someone who cares," Maya said.

Now, most guys would have taken that as a signal to depart. Well, most guys probably would have departed when she pushed them off her lawn.

But I noticed that Maya was still standing there. Sure, her back was to me. But she didn't move. Which could be a good sign. That's how desperate I was. So I decided to talk to her back.

"What happened was, all of a sudden there was this icon on my computer. It sent me to this private chat room. And these guys were talking about majorly bad stuff."

Slowly, she turned around. She gave me a long stare. "Are you yanking my chain, Kincaid, or are you serious?"

"Serious as mono," I swore. "Do you think you could have accidentally transferred someone's icon onto my hard drive?"

Maya frowned. "Anything is possible. Glitches happen. It's the first rule of computer land."

"How many computers have you worked on?"

"Lots," Maya said. "The business really took off. You'd be surprised at how many people don't understand the most basic things. I've tweaked a bunch of systems for kids at school, and even some businesses in town. Maybe thirty, forty clients."

She sat down on her front steps. After a second, I sat down, too. She didn't kick me off, so I figured that was good sign number two.

"Thirty or forty," I said. "That means it would be really hard to trace. Do you know your clients' e-mail addresses?"

Maya shook her head. "No reason to."

I sighed. "Too bad."

Maya leaned toward me, so close I could smell her soap. Which didn't smell like Tide, you might be surprised to hear. It smelled like . . . lilacs, or grass, or something. Maybe I was smelling the lawn.

"What are these people talking about?" she asked, real low.

I hesitated. Now that it came down to it, I wasn't sure how much to say. I had to admit that it would be a relief, at this point, to unload. But tell all to Maya Bessamer? She wasn't exactly Oprah. She wouldn't hold my hand and tell me I was brave to come forward. She'd call me an airhead again and tell everyone what a feeb I was. Jessica Manderly would probably fall off her seat in Mr. Pogue's class when Maya filled her in on my latest example of stupidity.

"Come on, Kincaid," Maya said impatiently. "Obviously, you're spooked. Spill it."

"I've got to swear you to serious secrecy," I said.

"Sure," Maya said.

"No, *I mean it*," I said.

I guess I kind of snapped at Maya, because she gave me a weird look. She didn't know whether to be mad at me or not. But after a second, she nodded. "Okay," she said. "I swear."

So I spilled. I told Maya everything, in order, right from the very first night. I didn't jump all over the place, like I had with the police and the FBI. I explained about the numbers that seemed like phone numbers but weren't. About how I remembered the chapter from *Johnny Tremain*. I even took the book out of my backpack and showed it to her. I told her about getting the paperback copy from the bookstore. About the police, and the FBI.

I couldn't read her expression at all. She just sat on the stoop. She didn't even nod, or gasp, or lift an eyebrow. And she leaned forward a little so that her hair was covering most of her face. I couldn't tell if I'd made any headway at all.

Finally, I finished. Maya was silent.

So I just waited for her to call me a cotton candy bleached-blond airhead again. That would be a treat.

"Wow," Maya said. "That's the most incredible story I've ever heard."

Sarcasm again.

Oh, well. I tried. I let out the breath I didn't realize I was holding. Maya Bessamer was about to cut me up and have me for breakfast. Well, why should I sit around and take it? I started to get up.

"No, Kincaid," Maya said. She put her hand on the knee of my jeans for a minute, then quickly took it off. "I mean it. It all makes sense. I hate to admit it, but it does."

Slowly, I sank down again. "It does?"

"Well, it's possible," Maya said slowly. "I mean, if it isn't true, it's an awfully big coincidence, isn't it? That the numbers correspond to letters that spell out the towns that had bombings?"

"That's what I think," I said.

"I can't believe you worked out the code," she said. "That was really smart of you."

"You know, you could make a big attempt not to sound *so* surprised," I said.

"I was born in this country, but I *am* half-Vietnamese," Maya said. "So I know about prejudice. I'd really like to help you nail these guys. What do you say to a partner?"

"*You?*" I blurted. I didn't intend to sound so mean. I was just surprised. But Maya lifted her chin and her eyes flashed.

"Yes, me," she said. "Because unlike you, I

have a working brain. I'm not orbiting the planet half the time."

"Let me get this straight, Bessamer," I said. "Is this the way you charm folks into doing what you want? By insulting them?"

"Look, Kincaid," Maya said. "It sounds like you need someone who knows computers. And you just might need some additional brain cells working on this one. Where would Mulder be without Scully? Holmes without Watson? Clark without Lois?"

"Fred without Wilma?" I said.

She smacked me on the leg. I'm telling you, you'd be surprised how much power this girl could pack.

"What do you say?" she asked. "Do you accept my offer?"

I hesitated. But to tell you the truth, I was relieved. It would be cool to have a partner. Especially someone as smart as Maya Bessamer. But I couldn't let her think I was wild about the idea. I know girls. She'd use it like a club.

I shrugged. "Sure. Whatever."

"Whoa," Maya said. "For a surfer dude, that counts as, like, a ringing endorsement."

She held out her hand, and I shook it. Her hand practically disappeared in mine.

"What now?" I said.

Maya frowned, thinking. "Let me ask you a few questions."

Then, before my eyes, Maya Bessamer turned into a district attorney. She fired off question after question at me, her laser-beam eyes forcing me to remember every detail.

How many were in the chat room group? What kinds of things did they say? Did PAT.riot73 always give out the number at the same time? Did it seem as though he was the leader? Could I tell where anybody lived? Did they ask me about myself? Did I think they'd try to recruit me?

Why did the girl bother having a computer? She already had a mega-RAM model for a brain.

Finally, she was done. Then she sat quietly for a minute.

Just when I was about to nod off, she picked up the brown bag again. She fished inside and took out the plastic fork. She broke off one tine, then held the broken fork up in front of my face.

"No, thanks, I already ate," I said.

"No, Kincaid," Maya said impatiently. "This is our strategy."

"Our strategy is a broken fork?"

She rolled her eyes. "A three-pronged attack," she said. She pointed to the first tine of the fork. "First, we go over my client list. If I accidentally transferred that icon, there's only one logical conclusion—someone in the chat group lives in Bunnington Beach."

"Which is my point, remember?" I said, a little annoyed.

"I'm just summarizing," Maya said. "Don't be so touchy." She pointed to the second tine. "Second, continue to monitor the group—let's call them the X Posse. Maybe they'll try to recruit you. We can trade off different nights. I'll pose as you."

"Me? You?"

"Absa-tively, dude," Maya said with a smirk. "I'm severely stoked at the whole concept, man."

"Don't forget that they think I'm a race car mechanic."

Maya rolled her eyes. "I know, it's a guy thing. But I can handle it. You have to admit you've been getting bored listening to that Patriot guy all night. You might miss something. Anyway, best-case scenario is that we catch the next number code, break it, and then warn the police in the town that's targeted."

"I already figured that's what I'd do," I said. Maya was getting awfully bossy all of a sudden.

I yawned, just to let her know that I wasn't

buying her Commander Bessamer act. But she poked me with the fork.

"Am I done yet?" I snapped.

"Overdone," Maya shot back. "Listen up, Kincaid. Here's the third prong. And it's the most tricky—bait and trap."

"Hold it. Translation, please."

"We've got to dangle some bait in order to catch the local guy," Maya explained.

"What kind of bait?" I asked.

"I don't know yet. We'll have to be careful, though. Because these guys are dangerous. If they suspected you . . ." Maya's voice died away. Then she snapped the plastic fork in two.

"Gee," I said. "Thanks for the visual aid."

"But first, we'll concentrate on prongs one and two," Maya said decidedly.

So, she was bossy. I won't argue the point. But it was good to have someone on my side.

We sat, watching the tiny lizards rove over Maya's lawn. Watching the ants swarm over the crumbs left from a cookie. Ah, Florida.

"So *is* Josh's mother's shrimp salad the best?" I asked.

"Are you kidding?" Maya said. "I would never eat it. It's been in Josh's backpack all day."

9//the bessamer engine

Maya packed more energy into five feet than I could muster up with a whole extra eight inches. She got more done before breakfast than I managed in a week. Then she'd fix me with those sharp dark eyes, and pretty soon I was hauling, too.

First, she printed out a list of all her clients. Next to each name was an exact description of everything she'd done to their computer. And next to that were notes on everything that Maya could remember them saying. She called it their "criminal profile."

The only trouble was, they weren't criminals. They were high school students. Parents. Local businesspeople. And the local homeless shelter.

Not exactly the FBI Most Wanted List.

Maya did some cyber-wizardry and found out the address of the chat group. Now she had her own icon on her computer. We thought it would be suspicious if Maya hung around the chat room, too. So we switched off nights monitoring. After three nights, Maya had to admit that I was right—this crowd was definitely living in Coma Land.

On Thursday, Maya brought over the file to my house after school. We sat on the front porch and went over it together, one more time.

We had already been able to eliminate a few names, since Maya hadn't fussed around with their hard drives. She'd just installed software, or had given them a basic computer lesson.

This time, we went over the list of students with a fine-tooth comb. Name after name. Bunnington Beach was pretty small, and I'd been in school with lots of these kids since kindergarten. I couldn't imagine any of them being involved in hate crimes.

After I'd said, "It can't be him," for the tenth time, Maya threw down the list.

"Kincaid, you can't eliminate every name on this list," she said. "It's got to be *somebody*."

"Okay," I said. "How about Josh Fallows?"

"Don't be ridiculous."

"Why not?"

"Because," Maya said, exasperated. "He bakes *cookies*, for heaven's sake."

"Hitler baked cookies," I said. "So what?"

"He has a crush on me, Kincaid," Maya said.

"He's asked me out about ten times. And in case you haven't noticed, I'm half-Vietnamese. What kind of a member of a hate group would get a crush on someone who's half-Asian?"

"Someone who's confused," I said.

She rolled her eyes.

I lay back on the wicker couch and tossed a ball up in the air and caught it. "There's something creepy about that guy."

Maya frowned. "There is not."

I caught the ball. "Is, too."

"Is not."

"Too."

"Not—will you cut it out, Kincaid! Now you have *me* talking like a three-year-old!" Maya scratched off Josh's name.

"This could take forever," I complained. I threw the ball up and it hit the ceiling, barely missing the light.

"And you could destroy the porch," Maya agreed.

"Let's face it," I said. "Nobody at Bunnington High would know as much history as Patriot73. But you should see JamminGuy's spelling mistakes. You could finger about half of the graduating class, easy."

Maya waved her pen in the air. "I have a theory. It's the salt air. I think a person's IQ goes

down in proportion to geographical proximity
to and amount of time spent on—a beach."

Maya pointedly glanced at my Boogie board,
which was leaning against the wall.

"LOL, Bessamer," I said. "You're a regular
comedian, aren't you."

Maya smirked at me, then turned back to the
list. "Maybe we should check out member pro-
files in the big online services to see if we can
match names with e-mail addresses," she said.

"Okay," I said, tossing the ball again.

"Are you going to come up with an idea, or
just keep agreeing to mine?" Maya complained.

"I'm thinking," I said.

"That must be a strain," Maya said.

"I can handle it," I said. I tossed the ball up
again, and she reached over and snatched it out
of the air.

"How about the third prong of the plan?"
she asked. "Did you come up with any ideas for
bait?"

"I used to mash a little bologna on a hook,"
I said. "Or once, I used this Dorito-paste. You
chew for a long time—"

Maya shuddered. "We have to dangle something really hot," she said. "So the leader will
tell the local guy to check you out in person."

I gulped. "In *person*? Whoa. Hold the phone.

As a matter of fact, hang the thing up. When you said 'bait,' I didn't think you meant *me*."

Maya ignored me. "Tell me again about when you told them about your job. What did you say, exactly?"

"The usual stuff. How I worked on the engines, fueled the cars, and stuff. Patriot was totally into it. He started asking me if a race car uses regular fuel. I told him that it was a higher octane. I figure it must be true, but I have never really been into racing, or cars, for that matter. He had me on the spot."

"I hope you didn't blow your cover," Maya said in an absentminded way. The girl could rag on me without even trying.

"I'd like to remind you that *I'm* the one who's been stringing these guys along," I said. "I was doing perfectly fine without—"

"You know, we have the advantage here," Maya interrupted. "Think about it. You never said what town you lived in. He knows you live in Florida, but since you said you worked at a racetrack, he'd figure Daytona, right?"

"Maybe."

Maya pushed her spiky bangs out of her eyes. "Definitely. So we know he lives here, but he doesn't know we know. You know?"

"I guess."

"Listen to me, Kincaid." Maya's dark eyes gleamed behind her glasses. "The *fuel*. What's high octane good for?"

"Making race cars go really fast," I said. "And—"

"Firebombs," we said together.

"So you dangle your access in front of them," Maya explained. "Real casual. Not like you think they're making bombs. More like a guy-to-guy thing. Like, if anybody wants to make their Toyota really roar, you can get your hands on some stuff."

I sat up. "That's a severely excellent idea. Then they could e-mail me—"

"—and if you get a response, we'll know who the local member is," Maya filled in. "Then you could arrange a meeting."

Both of us suddenly went real quiet. The logical question "What happens then?" was probably pinging around Maya's brain just like it was in mine. Were we getting ourselves into a situation way over our heads? Who did we think we were, the *Mission: Impossible* force?

The expression on my face must have looked a tad weaselish, because Maya said, "You wouldn't have to actually *talk* to the guy, Kincaid. You could just go to the meeting place. I could be around, hiding, and I'd probably recognize whoever it was, since we figured they were a client of mine, right? I'll give you some sort of signal as soon as I see him coming. And we can take off and go to the FBI."

It sounded like an okay plan. But, still. What if the guy surprised us? I didn't exactly feel comfortable with the idea of chatting with a mad bomber.

"I thought you were serious about catching these guys," Maya said impatiently. "No pain, no gain."

"Well, if you get me killed, I hope you organize a really nice funeral," I said.

Just then, Mom popped her head out the window right over my shoulder. I must have jumped three feet off the couch.

"Grace under pressure, Kincaid," Maya murmured. Then she gave Mom a big smile.

Mom gave that Mom-smile, which said, *Isn't it wonderful that my son has found such a nice friend?* It gave me the creeps.

"Maya, would you like to stay for dinner? I'm making roast chicken and corn bread."

"That sounds delicious, Mrs. Kincaid," Maya said. "But I don't know . . ."

Mom gave me a significant look. Obviously, I was supposed to recite some page out of *Miss Manners.*

"Uh, you might as well stay," I said.

Mom raised an eyebrow at me. I guess I wasn't exactly enthusiastic.

"Well, okay," Maya said. "Thank you, Mrs. Kincaid." As soon as Mom pulled her head back in the window, Maya said, "That was really nice of your mom."

"NBD," I said.

"What?"

"No big deal," I said. "She likes to feed people."

Maya looked hurt for a minute. She did this kind of wincing thing with her face.

"Anyway, if I stay, I can monitor the X Posse with you after dinner," she said.

"And here I thought you were staying for my sparkling dinner conversation," I said.

"And we can dangle the bait," Maya added.

I gulped. "So soon?"

"Why wait?" Maya pointed out.

"Right," I said. "Why wait." No way was I going to let Maya know that my blood had just run cold. Like, at subzero temperatures.

"And there's one more thing, Kincaid," Maya said.

What next?

Maya raised one eyebrow in that way she had. "Hitler did not bake cookies," she said.

10//high octane

It might surprise you to know that Maya was a big hit with my family. Mom kept giving her second helpings, and Maya just packed it away. Rosie stared at her with adoration from the moment Maya sang the whole chorus of "If I Only Had the Nerve."

And Dad was just overcome that I actually knew someone who could string a few sentences together without using the word "awesome." He practically foamed at the mouth when he discovered that Maya has a brother at MIT.

And it turned out that Maya's mother was the "girl" I'd seen Maya talking to on her front lawn. She is a sculptor who works with granite and marble.

"Whoa," I said. "That's what was on your front lawn. I thought it was a pile of rocks."

"Have some more chicken, Randy," Mom said hurriedly. Maybe she was hoping that if she kept my mouth full, I wouldn't say something stupid. Again.

"It's okay, Mrs. Kincaid," Maya said, shoveling in the mashed potatoes. "It does look like a pile of rocks."

Everyone laughed, and Mom looked relieved. Too relieved. And Dad was smiling way too broadly.

Suddenly, I got it. They thought that Maya Bessamer was my *girlfriend*!

Whoa. Talk about major miscommunication!

My fork clattered against my plate. "We'd better get going, Maya. It's almost seven-thirty."

"We have time," Maya said. She turned to my mom. "Randy and I are meeting someone online. But I have time to do the dishes."

"Don't be silly," Mom beamed. "You kids run along. It's Mr. Kincaid's turn."

"That's right," my dad said heartily.

Obviously, my parents were bonkers for Maya. My dad doing the dishes? That happened about once a century.

I got up to go. Tomorrow, I'd set them straight about thinking I'd fallen for a snippy, sarcastic know-it-all with glasses who didn't know the difference between speed metal and power punk. But, tonight, we had work to do.

The X Posse was already chatting when we entered the room. Maya and I just lurked for a while, waiting for an opening.

There was the usual boring chitchat. Probably as soon as they saw my address posted, they downshifted into dullsville. Maya and I waited for about a half hour. Then JamminGuy started jawing about some car he was trying to sell, only he wanted to sell it to the *right people*. Maya thunked me in the ribs with her pencil.

"There's your opening," she said. "Quick!"

So I typed out:

If you want to sell that Nova, you could make that baby rock with some high octane. I can get my hands on it, if you're interested.

PAT.riot73 stepped in then.

Sounds like you could get caught, friend. Word to the wise.

And I replied:

No way. They keep the stuff locked up, but I have a key. Taking it would be cake.

Then JamminGuy stepped in.

Thanks for you're offer. I live too far from Florida, anyways. Mabe when I retire.

Maya rolled her eyes at Jammin's spelling, but she said, "Great. We know Jammin isn't our local guy."

"If he's telling the truth," I pointed out.

Maya nodded. "True. Well, the hook is dangled. Let's hope someone bites."

"So long as they don't bite me," I said.

The next morning, I turned on my laptop even before I got out of bed. It was on the floor, and I just leaned over and switched it on.

"You've got mail!" my mail program sang out.

It was from the mostly silent 60.MAN:

Sounds like you have something to sell that I might be interested in buying. Can you get to a town a half hour south of Jacksonville?

I e-mailed back:

No sweat. Tell me where and when, and I'm there.

I hurried through breakfast, wolfing down my muffin and banana.

"Where's the fire?" Dad asked.

Some choice of words. "I have to meet Maya before school," I said.

"Oh," Dad said. He looked at Mom over the paper. She smiled.

I really had to clue them in on the fact that Maya was barely a friend, let alone a girlfriend. But I didn't have time.

I raced to school to tell Maya. I had printed out the mail, and handed it to her by her locker.

"This is fantastic," Maya said. "A half hour south of Jacksonville. That means he's setting up a meeting right here in Bunnington Beach. We've got him, Kincaid!"

"Almost," I said. "He has to follow through and set up the meeting."

"He will," Maya said. "I can feel it."

"I brought my laptop to school," I told her. "I can plug in my modem here in the lab."

"Why don't you do it now?" Maya suggested. "He might have responded already."

We hurried upstairs to the computer lab. I plugged in and fired up the old modem, and sure enough, my mailbox flag went up.

Maya clutched my arm. "Go ahead," she whispered.

I clicked on the mail icon, and I saw that the message was from 60.MAN.

How about 11:45 tonight at the Beachway Diner on SR 44 and Royal Palm Drive? Just in time for the graveyard shift. Sit in the last booth on your right.

"I know where that diner is," Maya said. "It's in an industrial neighborhood. My mom has a studio there."

"Why did he say the graveyard shift?" I asked nervously.

"A graveyard shift starts at midnight, I

think," Maya said. "We can ride our bikes there. It's not too far."

"But why would he *say* the graveyard shift?" I persisted.

"I don't know," Maya said. "It's just an expression, I guess. It doesn't matter. It's about a twenty-minute bike ride. It will be kind of creepy at night."

"You're telling me," I said.

We looked at each other. An empty industrial neighborhood was not exactly ideal. Too much could go wrong.

"Maybe I should e-mail back and suggest another time and place," I said. "Number one, it's way past my curfew."

"And B, you're grounded," Maya said. "I know." Then she punched me. Man, she was bionic. "Don't be a wimp."

"I'm not being a wimp," I protested. "I'm just being pract—"

"We can sneak out," Maya interrupted. "NBD, right?"

I just stared at her. She probably weighed about ninety pounds dripping wet. And here she was, raring to go toe-to-toe with a terrorist.

Well, if she could, I could.

"No big deal," I said.

11//jitters

It was surprisingly easy to sneak out of my house. My parents are both early-to-bed people. Even on Friday nights, they usually hit the hay around ten o'clock and fall asleep reading in bed. They aren't exactly party animals.

Maya didn't have a problem, either. Her bedroom is on the first floor, so she just climbed out her window.

It was a long bike ride out over the railroad tracks to the north part of town. Out there are a bunch of seedy-looking houses and big warehouse buildings that look totally spooky at night. I was actually relieved to see the lights of the Beachway Diner.

The place had that American grease-pit quality from the outside. It was one of those old diners from the early sixties, I guess. Someone had tried to spruce it up with pink paint on the trim. They must have gotten a deal on the paint, because it was the ugliest shade of pink you ever saw. I could just see them walking into Home Depot and asking for "something in the Pepto-Bismol range." Which is not a product an eating establishment would want to bring to mind, if you ask me.

We cycled past the diner, then locked our bikes to a sign a couple of blocks away.

"Okay," I said. "Let's go over the plan one more time. You go in first. You sit at the counter all the way to the left. Then you check out the place and make sure that you don't recognize anyone. If you do, you get coffee to go and split right away. I wait here for five minutes. Then I come in and go to the last booth on the right. You watch the street. When you see someone familiar, you give me the high sign, and I walk out."

Maya nodded. "Hopefully, he or she won't recognize you."

"Right. Or you," I said.

We both had baseball caps on. Maya had tucked her hair up inside it and pulled the brim way down over her forehead. In the cap and her denim jacket and jeans, Maya looked like a boy. We were counting on the fact that 60.MAN, whoever he or she was, wouldn't recognize her. Maya was so engulfed in denim that *I* could barely recognize her.

"You slip out when you can," I said. "And we meet back here. It's a foolproof plan, right?"

"Check," Maya said. "You scared?"

"Nah," I said.

"Me, too," Maya said. She grinned.

I pulled down the brim of her cap a little more. "Get going," I said. "And be careful, will you?"

Maya nodded. I watched her head down the block and walk slowly up the stairs to the entrance. The the door *swooshed* behind her.

I waited five minutes. Each minute felt like an hour. Then I followed her inside.

The bright lights made me blink for a minute. At least on the inside the place looked clean and almost cheerful. The upholstery was cracked and old, but the chrome shone and colorful signs advertising specials were hung over the grill. The place was deserted, except for a beefy guy drinking coffee and reading a newspaper. Maya sat on a stool at the very end of the counter, close to the side door.

I hesitated for a minute. When 60.MAN had told me to sit in the last booth on my right, did he mean on the right from the front door, or from the side door? Most people came through the side door, since that's where the parking lot was.

I wished I could consult with Maya, but she was ordering tea from the only waitress. So I just turned to my right and walked all the way to the end of the row of booths.

I ordered coffee from the waitress. I didn't really like coffee, but it seemed like the thing to do.

I looked at the menu, but I wasn't hungry. The thought of a cheeseburger just wasn't too tempting when I was waiting for a mad bomber. On the left side of the menu there were all these Asian specialties, like spring rolls and shrimp with basil and mee krob, whatever that was.

I hunched over my coffee. I kept glancing out into the dark street. When I got tired of that, I watched the clock over the grill. The waitress refilled my cup.

The clock hands kept turning. Eleven-fifty. Eleven-fifty-five. Straight up, twelve o'clock midnight. Five after twelve. And nobody showed up. I was starting to have severe caffeine jitters.

Suddenly, at about 12:10, customers started to pour in. It started out as a trickle and turned into a stream. Some of them sat at the counter, and some groups went into booths. They all asked for tea and ordered without looking at the menu, as though they came here all the time.

And they were all Asian.

I overheard the group in the next booth, talking about work, and I realized that they all must be factory workers. They'd just gotten off their shift.

The graveyard shift. Just like 60.MAN had said.

I took a sip of my coffee. It was cold. My stomach was clenched in about a million knots. Something was weird. Something was wrong. I looked over at Maya, and she lifted one shoulder in a shrug. She didn't know what to do, either.

My hands were shaking, and I put them in my lap. There was a long tear in the upholstery next to my leg. I guessed it was expensive to fix something like that. Somebody had covered it with duct tape, and I started picking at it nervously.

I was so jittery, I didn't realize that I'd unfastened half the tape until it was too late. I quickly started to smooth it down before the waitress came back over. But she was too busy filling orders right then.

That's when I noticed that the tear went all the way down to the floor. And it was a straight tear, as though someone had split the upholstery with a penknife. Weird.

I heard the chatter of a language I didn't understand. And the same words kept drumming in my head, over and over.

The graveyard shift. The graveyard shift.

I leaned down, disappearing below the table, to peel off the rest of the tape.

I bent the vinyl upholstery back.

Underneath the seat of the booth was a hollow space. Resting on the floor, I could clearly see a small canvas tote bag.

Now who, I wondered, would rip open the upholstery of a booth in order to secrete their bag underneath the seat?

I didn't have to ask the question. The answer had danced along my nerves and jump-started my heart.

Someone planting a bomb.

Was it possible? Was I caught in a trap?

The Asian voices pounded in my ears. I couldn't understand what they were saying, but I imagined them saying "graveyard, graveyard" over and over.

I came back up, slamming my head on the bottom of the table. I didn't even feel it. I fell out of the booth and shot to my feet.

"Everybody out!" I shouted. "Move fast!"

Nobody moved. Maya looked at me, her eyes wide.

"It's a bomb!" I said. "Just move!"

I reached into the booth next to me. A middle-aged woman with gray hair stared fearfully at me. I grabbed her and pulled her to her feet. Then I grabbed the younger woman who'd been sitting with her. I started pushing them toward the door.

"Now!" I yelled. "Hurry!"

Maya sprang to her feet. She tugged at the man reading the paper next to her. She helped up an elderly man who was busy slurping up soup. "Hurry!" she urged. Then she said some words in Vietnamese. Some of the people must have understood her, because they jumped up.

It seemed like we were moving in slow motion, but within seconds, everyone was hustling for the doors.

Maya opened the side door, and I reached the front. I kept it open while people streamed out, running now, fear in their faces.

The young Asian cook was the last to run out the door. His cap fell off. He stooped down to get it, and I said, "No time!"

I pushed him in front of me, and we started running, fast, following the others down the street. I saw Maya ahead, helping an older woman. The sky was dark, and the streetlights glittered on the blue-black concrete. Everything seemed to be happening slowly and fast, all at once.

And then the explosion came.

BOOM!

I felt it against my body. My spine seemed to compress against my chest. Next to me, the cook hit the dirt.

"Holy cow," the cook breathed into the tar.

I turned. With the heat on my face, I saw the flames. I couldn't breathe.

"Randy, move back." It was Maya, tugging at my sleeve. "Move back."

Her words came to me from far away. I looked down at her face. Her eyes were so wide and dark. I could see orange flames reflected in her glasses.

Together, we helped the cook stand up. We backed away, down the street, not taking our eyes from the burning diner.

The customers crowded onto a small area of pavement. Some of them had their arms around their neighbor. Some of them were crying.

Maya and I turned and faced the flames again. Behind us, we heard cries, we heard moans. Ahead of us, we heard the crackle of flames and a sudden *whoosh* as another small explosion took place. Suddenly, everything was way too real. I reached out and took Maya's hand.

12//waffles

It didn't take long for us to hear the sirens. We collapsed on the curb and sat, watching the fire burn. Even from hundreds of feet away, we could feel the heat.

I felt scared and numb, all at the same time. I think Maya must have felt the same way, because she actually leaned against me.

Her voice was muffled, and I had to bend over to hear her. She had lost her baseball cap somewhere, just like I had. Her hair felt soft against my cheek.

"I never really believed we were on the track of a terrorist group," she said. "I mean, I believed it. But I didn't *believe* it."

"I know," I said against her silky hair. It was so soft. It felt so good.

She pulled away and faced me. "This is really happening, Randy. It's really happening!"

A shudder rolled through her. I put my arm around her and pulled her against me again. I held her as tight as I could without hurting her.

"It's okay," I said. Even though it wasn't.

"What if he's here somewhere?" Maya said in a shaky voice. "What if he's watching us?"

I looked around the dark street. Suddenly, every shadow seemed as though it could dissolve into the form of a stranger.

A white news van turned the corner up ahead. It slowed when it passed the diner. Then, like a trolling trawler, it cruised down the street past us. It turned around and stopped.

"It didn't take them long," Maya said.

"They probably listen to the police band radio," I said.

Then the sirens grew louder, and the first engine screamed around the corner. The revolving yellow light flashed across our faces and hurt our eyes. Firefighters jumped out and began unrolling a hose. Another engine pulled up, and behind it, a police car.

Then an ambulance, siren screaming, lights flashing, careened down the street from the opposite direction. It pulled up near us. Two paramedics leaped out.

The dark street had come alive. The paramedics started moving through the crowd, checking to see if anyone was hurt. I waved a guy away from me and Maya and pointed to the elderly man lying with his head in a woman's lap.

Down the street, another news van lurched around the corner. It stopped in front of the fire, and a guy with a camera on his shoulder got out. A policeman hurried down to deflect it, and the guy jumped in the van again. It headed for us, and I could see the camera sticking out the window, shooting us.

The other policeman started to question the cook and the waitress. My arms tightened around Maya.

"I think we should split," I said next to her ear. "The police won't believe us, let's face it. It's better if we go to the FBI."

Maya nodded. We stood up, then melted back into the shadows. No one noticed us in the confusion. It was easy to slip out of the circle of light.

We kept backing away. We avoided the cop cars, the news truck, and the paramedics. We turned our backs on the fire. And we ran.

I knew I'd never be able to sleep.

I knew that when I closed my eyes, I'd only see licking flames and black ash. I knew that I'd only think about all those people, and Maya, and me, and what could have happened if I hadn't been nervous and picked at a piece of duct tape.

I lay in bed with my reading light on and stared at my room, at all the stuff I had, action figures and computer games and my old baseball card collection. It all looked as though it belonged to someone else now.

The house was so quiet. I wished Maya was with me. Which should tell you just how scared and lonesome I felt.

What I really wanted to do was wake up my parents and tell them everything. Or tell them I'd had a bad dream, like a little kid.

But I couldn't tell my parents. Not yet, anyway. They deserved at least one more night of sleep before I unloaded my latest stupid caper on them. I felt very grown-up at that moment. "Let them sleep," I said out loud.

Somewhere around three A.M., I decided to list in my head every CD in my collection, starting with the first one I bought.

I was trying to remember the name of Skull Fracture's second album when I fell asleep.

Sunlight poured into the kitchen the next morning.

"Hey, sleepyhead," Mom said over by the sink. "You sure slept in."

I mumbled something and grabbed the paper.

"Brunch on the porch this morning," Mom said. "It's a lovely day."

"Sounds great. I'm starving," I said mechanically.

The photograph took up the entire top of the front page. The diner was just a heap of twisted metal and charred beams.

DINER EXPLOSION AT MIDNIGHT.
ARSON SUSPECTED
POSSIBLE LINK TO NATIONWIDE BOMBINGS

There was a sketch underneath the photo. One of those police-composite things. I did a double take.

The guy looked exactly like me.

My blood chilled as I read:

Police Hunt Suspect

My knees gave way, and I sank down into a chair. Behind me, Mom hummed while she sliced pears. The sun made a buttery patch on the table and warmed my shoulders. But I was freezing. My knees were practically knocking together underneath the table. I tensed my muscles so they wouldn't shake.

The police had questioned everyone in the diner, especially the waitress and the cook. They all told the same story—how a "tall young man" stood up and warned them about a bomb, then herded them out the door.

And to make matters worse, there was "significant residue" left on the seat of the very booth I had sat in.

The police thought I'd had second thoughts. The police thought I was the bomber.

I looked at the sketch again. It made me look older, and mean, somehow. And they'd given me some stubble, even though I didn't have any.

But it was the same nose, the same light eyes. The same long hair that fell on my forehead and got into my eyes.

My dad came in the kitchen and looked over my shoulder.

"Friend of yours?" he joked. Dad was always jovial on Saturdays. He lived for his days off.

He leaned closer. "Hey, that guy looks like you, Randy. Or are *you* the mad bomber of Bunnington?"

He walked away, chuckling. I faked a laugh that sounded like a cross between a complaining cat and a choking lizard.

Then I grabbed the paper and headed out.

"Brunch in ten minutes!" Mom sang out.

"Mom, I'm not hungry," I said. "But thanks, anyway."

The phone rang as I was making a beeline for it. I snatched it up. It was Maya.

"Don't you think it's time we went to the FBI?" she asked. "Before you get arrested and go to jail for ten thousand years?"

"I'll be out in fifty," I joked.

Maya sounded nervous. "I mean it, Kincaid. They have to believe us now. I can't stand the pressure."

"Did you sleep last night?" I asked.

"Some. I finally had to do multiplication tables."

"I cataloged my CDs in my head."

Maya blew out a long breath.

"I'll be over in fifteen minutes," she said.

While I waited for Maya, I sat in the window seat of the living room and plugged in my modem. As soon as I was hooked up, an IM flashed on the screen. "Instant message." Maybe Maya forget to tell me something and didn't want to call back.

But it wasn't Maya. It was 60.MAN.

The words scrolled across my screen.

Don't be stupid, kid. Don't even think about the cops, or the FBI. Because we'll know. We're in your neighborhood. We know where you live. If you get too close to the flame, you get burned. And so does your family. Btw, those blueberry waffles sure look good. How can you resist?

I jumped back, as if my computer had burned my fingers. Then I leaped up and raced to the front porch.

My mom had set the table with one of those vintage tablecloths she likes. A blue jug held a bouquet of yellow flowers. My dad's hair was in that Saturday morning mussed-up state. My sister, Rosie, had her little fingers around the syrup pitcher.

Mom looked up and smiled at me. "Hi, honey. Change your mind?"

She held out a platter toward me. "Want a waffle?"

13//the lurker

I stood behind the curtain and looked out at the street. It looked normal. Quiet. Mr. Peterson was clipping his hedge. Timmy Davis was riding his bike up and down his driveway.

Everything looked normal, except that somebody, somewhere, was watching. Every window in every house seemed to wink at me, saying *I could be behind this curtain!* Every tree could be hiding a lurker. Every car with tinted windows could be concealing a threat.

Our house was a new Florida house. It had lots of open windows. Usually, we keep the front door wide open to catch the breeze. French doors have paned glass that would be easy to break.

And there are wood floors and wood beams and lots of filmy curtains. All the things that would go up in a second in a fire. All of the things that would burn.

Mom has this flexible schedule because she

takes Rosie into school every morning. She is usually here with Rosie when the mail comes. If she got a plain brown envelope, or a package, she'd tear it open. No reason not to. No reason in the world . . .

My skin was ice cold, but I was sweating. Now I couldn't go to the police. I couldn't go to the FBI. They knew who I was. And I knew from last night that these guys didn't bluff.

There were so many of them. And I was alone. Just then I looked out the window and saw Maya streaking down the street on her bike. She was wearing denim shorts, and her tan legs flashed as she pumped on the pedals, moving fast.

I watched her for a minute. I was suddenly so glad to notice all those things that irritated me about her, all those Boy Scout qualities. How determined she was, how smart, how brave.

And for the first time that day, I felt lucky. Maya Bessamer was my partner.

I headed out to the side yard to intercept her before she came up to the front porch and Mom stuffed a waffle in her mouth.

When she saw me, Maya bumped over the lawn and rolled to a stop near me. Her bangs stuck to her forehead with perspiration, and she pushed them away impatiently. "What's up?"

she said. "You look like a smashed palmetto bug."

"Things just got more complicated," I said. "We've *got* to find 60.MAN. Because he's found *me*."

Maya swung off her bike. She looked frightened. "What happened?" she asked.

Quickly, I filled her in on the message I'd received on my laptop. "It's not just a bluff, Maya. They know where I live. And they'll firebomb my house in a second if we go anywhere near the FBI or the police. My family will be toast."

Maya chewed on her lip. "It sure looks that way."

"They could have tapped my phone!" I said. "Who knows what they can access. If they can see blueberries in waffles, they can find out anything, Maya!"

"I have bad news, too," Maya said. "They changed their Internet address. We can't even lurk in the chat room anymore. They know that we're onto them. Obviously." She lowered her bike onto the grass and then sank down next to it. "But we have to do something, Randy. People could die if we don't."

Maya's face was pale. She had faint purple smudges under her eyes. "I keep thinking about those faces last night. That old woman and her granddaughter."

I looked over at the porch. Dad was just finishing clearing the table. Mom was relaxing with her second cup of coffee.

"But what about my family, Maya?" I said. "I know they're a pain, but I kind of like having them around. We can't go to the FBI now. I'd be putting them in danger."

"I know," Maya said.

Then Maya did a really nice thing. She reached up and slipped her small hand into mine. She squeezed my hand hard, then let it go.

She didn't have to say a word. She'd just told me that we were a team. Together. And we'd find a way.

"Okay," Maya said. "Let's attack this logically. How could he have found out where you live and who you are?"

"The only thing I can figure out is that he was there last night," I said. "Just like you said. He watched us. And then he followed us home."

Maya shuddered. I didn't feel too comfortable myself. Thinking about someone in the shadows, tailing us as we rode through the dark streets.

"The thing is," Maya said, "there was nobody around. Remember? The only people on that street were customers from the diner. It's an industrial neighborhood, so it clears out at night. There was nobody to come running when they heard the explosion. That was what was so spooky, in a way. It was like we were on the moon."

I sank down on the grass next to Maya. She was right. I hadn't thought about it before.

"He couldn't have been in the diner," I said. "He would have blown himself up. So he must have been hiding."

"But where?" Maya asked. "There really wasn't anyplace to hide. Think about it, Kincaid. No trees. No alleys. There weren't even awnings or entryways where he could hide."

"He could have been in one of the buildings," I said. "Looking out the window at us."

"That's true," Maya said. "But he'd have to be really quick. As soon as we started walking away, he'd have to be out the door and in his car. He couldn't have followed us on foot."

"It's possible, I guess," I said, thinking about it. "We walked slowly so we wouldn't attract attention. At least at first."

"So maybe we should check out the buildings around there," Maya said. "One of the names of the companies might sound familiar to me."

"Okay," I said. I felt better, knowing that we could start somewhere.

"It's strange, though," Maya said. "No cars were parked on that street, remember? It must have been parked down a side street. How could 60.MAN have been sure he'd have time to trail us to our bikes, then run to his car and follow us?"

"Maybe he parked near our bikes," I said.

"Which means he saw us before we went inside," Maya said. "But we were so careful! We left our bikes two blocks away."

"Maybe there was more than one guy staking the place out," I suggested.

We were going around and around. And we still hadn't figured anything out.

Maya stood up. "Well, we're not going to solve anything sitting here. Let's go check out those warehouses."

Maya came up with a great cover. Since her mother works in the area, she offered to hand-deliver invitations to her latest open studio to all the businesses nearby.

Maya's mother looked surprised at our offer when we dropped in on her at her studio. Now that I saw her up close, I could tell that she was older than a girl. But even dressed in overalls and a striped T-shirt, she was a knockout. And believe it or not, I could even see a slight resemblance to Maya.

"Sure, honey," she said. "Thanks for helping out. Nice to meet you at last, Randy."

I said I was glad to have met her, too. It's one of those things you have to say to people, even though you're thinking of a million other things. Normally, I would have been totally interested in prowling around the studio, which was filled with junk. Big hunks of stone, hammered copper, and big sketches pinned to the wall. I couldn't imagine tiny Mrs. Bessamer—or actually, Ms. Bui, since she had kept her maiden name—hauling around those slabs of marble. I guess bionic muscles ran in the family.

Maya and I each grabbed a stack of invitations and split. We started at the warehouse across the street from the diner and moved down the block. Across the street, the charred frames and twisted metal of the diner reminded us of the horrible night before. There were police barriers set up around the spot, and we could see a couple of men sifting through the debris. Probably looking for clues in order to nail me as the bomber.

"Don't look at it," Maya murmured. "And pull your cap down."

Sometimes the names of the businesses were posted outside, so we didn't have to ring the bell. We wrote down every name. Later, we'd check them out to see if any officers of the company had familiar names. We figured you'd have to be a manager or pretty high up in order to have keys.

Some warehouse buildings had offices for ten or more small businesses. We went to each office to drop off invitations. Then we'd try to see if there was an office directory on the wall, and scan the names.

We worked our way down the block, then back up again. We were hot and tired by the time we got to the last building.

And we'd found absolutely zilch.

We paused on the stoop outside the last building. Maya banged her fist against the brass railing.

"We have to find him," she said. "We have to turn the tables. Make *him* sweat the way he made *us* sweat. He threatened your family, Kincaid! How dare he do that!"

Right before my eyes, Maya had turned from a tired kid into an avenger. I sure wouldn't want to meet up with her in a dark alley.

"We have to think of some other way to figure out how he found you," Maya said. "I don't think he was hiding in a building, somehow."

"Maybe we could buy all the local papers and look at the photos," I said. It was kind of a lame suggestion, but I couldn't think of anything better. "Maybe we'd catch something in the background that would be a clue."

"It's worth a shot," Maya said. "But, wait a second. Maybe we can do even better."

"What do you mean?" I asked. I could tell the Bessamer bean was clicking away now.

"My brother's friend works at WBBU-TV," Maya said. "I bet he'd let us look at the uncut footage from last night. Remember how the news crews arrived so fast?"

"One of them even got there before the fire engines," I agreed. "That's a severely excellent plan, Bessamer. Let's go."

14//way up close and personal

"Hello, Heartbreak," Maya's friend Kent said.

No, he wasn't reciting a song lyric. He was greeting Maya.

Maya rolled her eyes. "Give it a rest, will you, Kent? This is my friend Randy."

Kent grinned at me. "Pleased to meet you."

Kent turned away to pick up a clipboard from his desk. "Why does he call you 'Heartbreak'?" I asked Maya in a low voice.

"Because he's an idiot," Maya growled.

When Kent turned back, he was grinning. "I'll tell you why, Randy. Because I happen to hang at the Bessamer house pretty often—"

"Actually," Maya broke in, "we're thinking of adding a wing just for Kent—"

"—So I happen to have a ringside seat at this gorgeous girl's habit of conquering every heart in sight," Kent finished. "Including mine. So you know I'll do anything for you, Maya. I think. By the way, what *do* you want?"

While Maya explained to Kent what we wanted, I checked him out. He was about five years older than me and a few inches taller. He had dark hair and blue eyes, and he smiled a lot. He seemed like a nice guy, but I hated his guts.

What was he talking about? Maya Bessamer, a *heartbreaker*? Jessica Manderly was a heartbreaker. And Samantha Pedraza—I'd crawl over broken glass just to open her Diet Pepsi. But *Bessamer*? All right, she's kind of cute. In her own way. But what kind of guy gets totally juiced over some tiny brain with glasses and a big mouth?

Other cyberheads with glasses, I guessed. Or lame-o cookie bakers like Josh Fallows. That made me feel better, for some reason.

Kent led us to one of the editing machines in a small office. He set up the tape from the night before, then showed Maya how to use the basic functions of the machine, like stop and rewind, freeze and zoom. I wished that Kent would freeze his attitude and zoom out of there. Did he have to be so nice to Maya? It was sickening.

Finally, he said he had work to do. I was sure glad to see the back of him.

"Let me know if you need me, Heartbreak," he told Maya.

"Don't hold your breath," I muttered.

"What's the matter with you?" Maya asked me after Kent shut the door. "Are you okay?"

"I'm cool," I said.

"Yeah, so you keep telling the world," she snapped. "Hang on to the delusion, Kincaid."

"Why don't you roll the tape?" I shot back. "I think Kent said to press play, if you can handle it."

Scowling, Maya pressed the button. We didn't say anything as the tape ran.

All my annoyance drained away as the fire burst on the screen. It all happened again, right before our eyes. The smoke, the fire, the fear, the look in people's eyes. We heard all the interviews, the crying, the bewilderment.

After it ended, I heard Maya swallow. Her voice was hoarse when she said, "Okay. Let's rewind and watch it in slow speed."

We looked at the footage more carefully. We stopped the tape every time the cameraman moved and set up another shot. Then we'd search the background, looking for a clue.

Suddenly, Maya let out an exasperated breath. She pushed away from the console and rolled backward on her chair. She hit the wall.

"This isn't getting us anywhere," she said,

disgusted. "We were already gone during this part. We split when the TV crews started to arrive. This was a dumb idea."

"It was worth a shot," I said.

"I guess we should just go."

"Poor Kent will be devastated," I said.

Maya gave me a look of scorn, then turned back to the frozen image. "I wish we could get the footage from that first TV station," she said. "The one that showed up before the first fire engine, remember? You can see the van on the first part of the tape. I couldn't catch the name of the station, though."

I nodded. "Me neither."

Then a major lightbulb went off in my brain. A thousand watter. "Let's roll it back again," I said.

"Why?" Maya said. "It's no use. And I'm hungry."

"Just once more," I said. "Trust me."

"Now that's an idea I have trouble getting behind," Maya muttered, but she rolled back and rewound the tape.

I watched the monitor carefully. This time, I didn't look at the background. I paid attention to the van.

"Do you notice anything funny, Maya?" I asked, pointing at the van.

She shook her head. "Nada."

"See right there—the driver cruises once past us, then stops. And before the other TV crew started filming, he'd already cruised past the diner, then past us, and stopped. Remember?"

"So?"

"So, *why didn't he stop and shoot the scene*? Why didn't he interview anyone?" I said. "What kind of a reporter goes to the scene of a big disaster and *doesn't get out of his car*?"

"A lousy one," Maya said. But she looked at the monitor, intrigued.

"Maybe if we zoom in, we can read that logo," I said.

I froze the image as the van half-turned. "Can you read that?" I said. "I think it says 'SunB.' And right below it 'Comm.' But that's all I can see. But in the other shot, we have a pretty good view of the license plate. Do you know how to look up license plate numbers? Maybe on the Internet, somehow? Or how good are you, Maya—could you hack into the DMV?"

But Maya wasn't listening. She was staring at the van. Then she pressed fast-forward. She jabbed at the stop button as the van turned again.

"There," she said. She pointed to the screen.

"See that logo? It's the rays of the sun."

I could just barely make it out. "I see it," I said. "That might help. We could draw up a list of all the local stations, and find out what their logos are—"

"We don't have to look up anything," Maya said softly. "Because I know who 60.MAN is."

15//stormy weather

"It's Jeff Yobel," Maya said. Her voice rose in excitement. "SunBelt Communications. He owns a cable TV station. But he made all his money from dry cleaning stores—Brite Day Cleaners."

"I know those cleaners," I said. "My mom uses them."

"See," Maya said, pointing to the screen. "S U N B is the beginning of 'SunBelt.' He probably has a press pass because of the TV station. It all fits. He hired me to work out an interface between his computer at home and his computer at work." Maya turned to me. "Right before I worked on your system."

I felt the hairs on the back of my neck prickle. "Looks like we've got our man."

Maya nodded. "So what do we do now?"

Maya and I kicked it around for a while. We couldn't go to the FBI yet. I didn't want to put my family in danger.

Besides, Maya pointed out that we didn't know for sure that Yobel was 60.MAN. We needed solid proof. Proof good enough so that if we went to the authorities, they'd slap Yobel in jail and nab every single member of the X Posse. Then they'd all be so busy calling their lawyers, they wouldn't have time for revenge.

Finally, we agreed to take a quick bike ride over to SunBelt and check it out. Maya was itching to get her little hands on Yobel's hard drive.

Maya said good-bye to the bonehead Kent, who called her "sweetheart" this time. The guy was running on my last nerve.

We rode our bikes to SunBelt Communications. It was a cinder block building that looked run-down. The familiar white van was in the parking lot. We crouched behind some bushes at the edge of the lot and stared at the building.

"What now?" I said.

"I don't know," Maya said. "It's Saturday, but he might be in there. Then again he might not."

"That's succinct," I said.

"Succinct?" Maya asked.

"Yeah, you know—to the point," I said.

"I'm not asking for a definition, Kincaid. I'm just surprised you knew the word," Maya said. She did that flicking thing she does with her hair.

She takes her index finger and just flicks one side of her hair back behind her shoulder while she grins at you. You could really learn to hate a girl like that.

"I bet you don't know the word I'm thinking of right now," I said.

"Shhhh," Maya said. "Look, that's his office right there. And the light is on."

I looked over at the building. From behind the glass of a high, small window, I could see a faint light.

"So he's in there," I said. Just then, a big drop fell on my forehead. "It's raining."

Maya looked up at the sky. "It's just a sun shower."

Then a huge black cloud blocked out the sun. I heard the rumble of thunder. "I suggest shelter," I said. "We can come back—"

"Just hang a minute, Kincaid," Maya said. "It's Saturday. Maybe he's working a half-day."

Lightning flashed, and Maya jumped. But she didn't take her eyes off the building. I looked uneasily at the tree we were standing under. One thing you learn in Florida is to always take shelter during a storm. You don't fool around with lightning.

"So that means we can come back," I said. "After the rain stops. And after lunch. There's a sandwich shop across the street. We could even get a table by the window and watch for the van."

"Okay," Maya said. She didn't move. "The lights just went out!" she hissed.

Ignoring the fat drops that were now plastering my T-shirt to my back, I peered through the rain.

"Duck!" Maya hissed.

I looked around, thinking she was calling my attention to a waddling bird, but Maya yanked on my T-shirt and pulled me down. I went *splat* into the dirt.

"Hey!"

"Chill, Kincaid. He's coming out," she told me. "He could recognize us."

I peered through the bushes. A man walked out of the building and ran through the rain to his van. He was a completely ordinary-looking person. He was fortyish and paunchy-ish and nerd-ish. If you put a hair net on Jeff Yobel, he could be flipping hamburgers in a fast-food joint. If you put a white coat on him, he could be cleaning your teeth. If you put a Frisbee in his hand at a picnic, he'd be the dweeby guy who'd throw it into the potato salad.

"He looks so . . . normal," I muttered.

"What did you expect, a guy with a sign

around his neck saying 'psycho'?" Maya whispered.

As soon as the van sped out of the parking lot, Maya stood up. "I'll be back in three minutes. Do you have a set of keys?"

"Keys?"

Maya put out her hand. I dug into the pocket of my jeans and put my key chain in her hand. Dangling from it was a pair of miniature Day-Glo orange high-tops.

"Classy," Maya said. She smoothed her wet hair and tucked it behind her ears. She tried to smooth out the wrinkles in her white cotton shirt. "How do I look?" she asked.

She looked like a drowned rat. "Stunning," I said. "What are you—"

"Be right back," she said, and bolted across the parking lot.

I stood and waited, trying to look nonchalant while the skies poured what felt like a bucket of water on my head.

Finally, I saw her heading out of the front door again. She ran toward me.

"How about that sandwich now?" she asked, tossing my key chain to me.

"What did you just do?" I asked.

"Let's get out of the rain first," Maya said. "Come on."

We headed across the street to the sandwich shop. I waited while Maya dried off her arms and legs with a napkin, then ordered the Momma Mia Super-Italian Sub. We got our sandwiches and took a seat by the window so we could see if Yobel came back.

"Are you going to tell me what's going on?" I complained as I took a bite of my roast beef.

She swallowed a huge bite. "It was simple. I told the receptionist that I'd worked on Yobel's computer last week, and I've been looking all over for some keys I lost, and could I check his office."

"You lost your keys for a week and didn't think to check there earlier?" I asked skeptically.

She shrugged. "People don't care about details like that. I just acted really spacey. Guess who I used as my role model?" she asked.

I pretended to ignore the insult, like it was beneath me. "So she let you in Yobel's office?"

Maya nodded. "She was watching a show on this little TV she had hidden in her drawer. She just waved me through. Of course, I didn't have time to really look, or check the files on his hard drive. She might have gotten suspicious if I had been in there too long. Besides, Yobel might have come back. He could have just gone to lunch or something."

"So what was the point?" I asked.

"I unlatched that window," Maya said. She took another enormous bite of her sandwich. "Now we have a way to break in," she said, chewing.

For a minute, I hoped I had misheard her. She had been chewing on a half-pound of salami, pepperoni, and ham, after all. "Break *in*?"

"Tonight," Maya said.

I put down my sandwich. "Okay, let's review. First of all, you can't fit through that window."

"Sure I can," Maya said. "I'm small. Haven't you noticed? I can fit."

"If you say so, Bessamer," I said. "But how are you going to get up to the window? A ladder?"

"Don't be silly. That would be way too conspicuous," Maya said, wiping at a blob of mustard on her lip with a napkin. "You're going to give me a boost. Then I'll come around front and unlock the door."

"But don't people work at night at a TV station?" I asked.

Maya shook her head. "It's a Podunk cable station," she said. "At night, they just run taped stuff. I remember from when I worked there at night. There was just one technician way in the back room. He won't hear us."

"You hope."

"Everything's a risk," Maya said. She put down her sandwich. "Look, Kincaid. We can't go to the FBI unless we have solid evidence. So unless you have any better ideas . . ."

"I don't at the moment," I said.

She waved her pickle at me. "Even if Yobel is smart enough not to have any incriminating files on his hard drive, at least we can access the X Posse from his computer. We can lurk."

"But won't they know we're listening?"

Maya said something, but her mouth was full of sandwich again. Let me tell you something. It's hard to plan a break-in with a hearty eater.

"What?"

She swallowed. "I said, trust me."

"Trust you?"

She smiled innocently. And, then, just when I looked away, the girl reached over and stole my pickle.

16//a world to come

It wasn't a dark and stormy night. But I wished it were. It was clear, and there was a full moon rising. Which is exactly the kind of weather conditions you *don't* want for a break-in.

The good news was, Mom and Dad actually canceled my grounding. They were so beside themselves that I was meeting Maya that they let me go if I was home by nine.

At least Maya was right about one thing: The SunBelt Communications building was dark. One small light burned in a back window, which Maya said was the studio.

We crossed the parking lot and stood underneath Yobel's office window. The lights were on in the parking lot. Between the moon and the streetlights, I felt as though I were center stage about to belt out "My Way."

"Okay," Maya said nervously. "Don't be nervous."

"I'm not nervous," I said.

"Right," she said. "Neither am I. Okay. We'll just do this very fast. Give me a boost, make sure I'm inside, then go to the front door."

Maya placed her slightly muddy sneaker in my hand. I gave her a boost. But I hadn't realized how light she is. I shot her up so fast she lost her balance. Her hands slapped against the wall of the building. She would have fallen, but I caught her around the waist.

"Thanks, Kincaid," she grunted. "You nearly sent me over the roof."

"Sorry," I said. My mouth was against her shirt. I had just enough time to register how small and delicate her waist was. My hands could have spanned it. I could feel the heat of her skin through her thin shirt.

Suddenly, I felt very spacey and confused. Nerves.

I lowered her down until her feet touched the ground.

"Okay, let's try again," Maya said. "Slower this time."

I boosted her up, and she balanced by clutching the top of my head. Then she kind of knelt on my shoulders while she leaned against the building and pushed open the window. Muddy sneakers waved in my face as I heard it squeak open.

"Here I go," she whispered.

She slithered in headfirst. Her feet kicked, and then disappeared. I heard a thump.

"Are you okay?" I whispered.

Her face appeared at the window. "Just get moving."

Keeping out of the streetlights' glare, I slinked around to the front. I waited a few seconds, nervously glancing around. It was only about seven-thirty, so cars were still driving by. But nobody gave me a second glance.

Maya opened the door a crack. "Hurry!"

I slipped inside. The reception area was dark, and I bumped right into Maya. "Sorry."

"It's okay." When she moved away, her hair brushed my chin. The smell of her shampoo wafted up. I sure picked the most peculiar moments to notice how good Maya Bessamer smelled.

"This way," Maya said.

I followed her down a short corridor to Yobel's office. Maya switched on the desk light.

"What about the tech guy in the back?" I asked.

"He's watching *The Brady Bunch* and laughing like a hyena," Maya said. "I checked."

She crossed to the computer and switched it on.

Within minutes, her fingers were clicking away at the keyboard. "First, I'll sign on as a guest online. Then, I'm going to create a new e-mail address," she explained. "Once I'm in the system, I can access the icon. I hope."

"I hope so, too," I said.

Maya typed and clicked and typed again.

The modem made those beeping scratchy noises. She typed and clicked some more, exited, and came back in again.

"Okay," Maya murmured. "Don't let me down, baby." Again, she clicked away. She talked under her breath as she worked, and finally let out a whole string of "come on come on come on come on." Then the icon popped up, she clicked on it, and we were in.

The familiar names popped up. PAT.riot73, JamminGuy, SwampFox, OffRoad66. And 60.MAN.

Maya's new e-mail address, AnyJdoe123, popped into the member's box.

Howdy, stranger, PAT.riot73 wrote. *Welcome to the group. We're talking about city planning issues right now.*

"That's their cover," I said.

Sounds interesting, Maya typed. *I'm an architect.*

I grinned. "That's the last thing they want

to hear. Somebody who actually knows what they're talking about."

"This is almost fun," Maya said grimly, and PAT.riot73 began to talk again.

I checked Yobel's clock. "If PAT.riot73 is going to give a clue, it'll be soon. It's almost seven forty-five."

So what do you build, AnyJdoe123? SwampFox asked.

Shopping malls, Maya typed out. *I see them as the cathedrals of the 21st century.*

She grinned. "I read that in an article."

A civilization gets the monuments it deserves, PAT.riot73 wrote.

"I hope he doesn't give the code," Maya said nervously. Her fingers tapped on the mouse pad anxiously. "What if we can't stop the bombing, Randy? We'll be responsible . . ."

"Look, 60.MAN just signed off," I said. "That means there probably isn't a bombing planned. He must know that."

Maya looked up at me. "Or he already knows the target."

Well, time to flap my wings and fly, PAT.riot73 wrote.

"This could be it," I said. "He always says time to go do something before he gives out the clue."

I put my hand on Maya's shoulder. I leaned over, closer to the screen.

As for the 21st century, I'm looking forward to the world to come, PAT.riot73 wrote.

"The World to Come!" Maya and I both burst out. By now, we knew every chapter title in *Johnny Tremain* by heart.

"Oh, no," Maya moaned. "They have another bombing planned."

"Here comes the code numbers," I said.

Here's the number you asked for, SwampFox—243 922–5383.

"You got that?" Maya asked.

I was already writing it down. "Got it. Don't exit yet. They might get suspicious."

Maya continued to chat with SwampFox and JamminGuy. I took out my copy of *Johnny Tremain* and turned to the "A World to Come" chapter. Then I began to count out the lines and letters.

I went as fast as I could, but I had to be careful. Maya kept spinning back and forth on the chair, making it squeak. It didn't do wonders for my concentration.

"Are you finished yet?" she finally asked, giving me a nervous glance over her shoulder. "I want to check out Yobel's files. And we'd better get out of here. We're pushing our luck."

"Go ahead and log off," I said. "I'm almost done."

And in another minute, I had it:

When you broke 243 922–5383 down into blocks of two numbers, you got: 24 39 22 53 83

When you took the first number as the line, and used the second to count off the letters in each word, you got: W I L L I

"Willi," I said. "That could be anything."

"We need a phone book, or an atlas," Maya said. "Wait, I can access one on the Internet."

She clicked a few times and found an atlas in the online service's reference section. She clicked on "Index" and moved quickly to the "W" section.

"Look at this," she breathed. "Williams, Arizona. Williamsburg, Virginia . . ."

"Williamsport, Pennsylvania. Williston, North Dakota," I read over her shoulder. And there were about six more towns after that.

Maya banged her fist on the table. "If only we could figure out the code for the state! What are we going to do, call up the police in every one of these towns and warn them?"

"What else can we do?" I said.

We exchanged a long glance. We knew we were taking a chance. If the X Posse found out . . .

But we couldn't let the bombing happen.

Maya nodded. "Let's do it from here, anonymously," she said. "At least if they trace the call, it will lead them to Yobel."

"Good idea," I agreed. "Can you look up police stations and sheriffs' numbers on the Internet?"

"Probably," Maya said. "Just give me a few minutes here." She hitched her chair up to the computer again.

It didn't take long. Starting with the first town in the atlas, we began calling.

Nobody believed us. The sheriff in Arizona asked if it was past my bedtime. The police officer in Williamsburg said of course he'd keep an eye out for a mad bomber. But I doubted his sincerity.

Maya blew out a breath, ruffling her bangs. "Who's next?"

"North Carolina," I said.

But just then, lights swept across the far wall of the office. Maya immediately reached over and snapped off the light. I hoisted myself up and peered out the high window.

The white van had pulled up at a hasty angle near the front door. And Jeff Yobel was heading for the entrance!

17//trapped

Maya looked around wildly. "What should we do?"

"You go out the window," I said. "Quick!"

I held my fingers together for a boost.

"But what about you?" Maya whispered. "You can't fit through that window!"

"I'll hide. Go!"

But Maya didn't move. "I'm not leaving you here with him, Randy."

What was the matter with the girl! When it came to stubbornness, she was the champ. "You're wasting time!" I hissed angrily. "Come on!"

"It's too late now, anyway," Maya said.

"That's because you're arguing with me!" I said.

But I knew Maya wouldn't budge. I looked around. The only thing I could think of was the obvious.

"The closet," I said.

I pulled Maya toward it. "The computer!"

she said. She ran back and switched it off.

We crowded into the walk-in closet together. It was stuffed with books, boxes, files, computer paper, a couple of shirts on a hanger, and a mildewed old raincoat. We inched behind the boxes and then flattened ourselves against the wall. I carefully slid the raincoat along the rack to hide us.

A few moments later we heard the office door open. We'd made it just in time.

We couldn't see Jeff Yobel. But we could hear him. We heard the office door close. We heard the chair creak. We heard him grunt, then open and close a desk drawer.

Then we heard numbers being punched on a phone. I could hear a muffled voice, but I couldn't make out words. I wanted to inch closer to the door, but there were too many things in the closet. I'd definitely make a noise, and I couldn't afford to take any chances . . . because we already knew that Yobel was perfectly capable of killing us if he found us.

I tried to lean just a bit closer to hear what he was saying. But my foot hit a duffel bag, making a soft *thud*. I heard Maya's indrawn breath, and I tensed. We waited, not daring to breathe. But there was no interruption of Yobel's voice in the next room. He hadn't heard it.

The thing was, my toe had hit something hard and metallic. And I wanted to know what it was. Slowly, carefully, I slid down until I was crouching.

The duffel was unzipped. I slid my fingers inside. I felt something cool. Metal. My fingers explored the shape.

A gasoline can.

Around it were rags and bottles and a bundle of wires. A clock.

And I knew what it was.

The makings of a homemade bomb.

Slowly, I raised myself up again. Maya looked at me questioningly. I pointed down to the duffel. Then I made a motion with my hands to indicate an explosion.

Maya gasped.

She realized what she'd done in less than an instant. Her hands flew to her mouth, and her eyes went wide with horror.

We heard the desk chair creak.

I put my fingers on the back of her neck and pushed her down. Together, we crouched behind the computer boxes. We rolled ourselves into the tightest balls that we could.

Footsteps approached the closet.

The doorknob turned. A slender bar of light widened as Jeff Yobel opened the door.

18//lives on the line

We didn't breathe. The bar of light kept widening. It illuminated the toe of Maya's sneaker.

Maya didn't see it. If I showed her, she'd yank her foot back. And if she did, Yobel would catch the motion out of the corner of his eye.

Just then, I saw Maya's gaze move down to the light on her foot. Her whole body stiffened. But she didn't move her foot.

Ninety-nine girls out of a hundred would have pulled their foot back, fast. Okay—guys, too. But Maya was incredible. A coolness factor of ten plus. She just closed her eyes for a split second. Then, slowly, silently, she began to withdraw her foot from the light.

Yobel took one step into the closet. Inches away from my face, his hand closed on the handles of the duffel bag. He swiped it off the floor with a grunt. Then he stomped out and shut the door.

Silently, Maya let out the breath she was

holding. I took a deep, quiet breath, then let it out again.

That was close. Way close. Too close.

The light underneath the door went out. The office door slammed.

He was gone. But we waited a good minute, counting off the seconds. At last, we crept out of the closet. I don't know about Maya, but my legs were shaky. I could barely hoist myself up to look out the window.

The parking lot was empty. Yobel was gone.

But where did he go?

"He's gone to the next target," Maya said. "What are we going to do?"

"I don't know. Maybe he left a clue."

I began searching the desktop.

"What are you looking for?" Maya asked. "A note saying, 'Gone to bomb North Dakota'?"

"I don't know what I'm looking for, Bessamer," I snarled. "Do you have any better ideas?"

Maya slid down the wall until she was sitting on the floor. "No," she said. "It's over, Kincaid. There's nothing more we can do."

She was right. There wasn't anything on the desk to tell us where he'd gone.

"Look, it has to be somewhere fairly close,"

I said. I perched on the edge of the desk and leaned over to talk to her. "Because we know it's tonight."

"What's the use?" Maya said.

"Maya, listen to me. We can't give up now. Look, we can eliminate California and North Dakota. It could be that town in Georgia, or the one in Alabama, if he's driving."

Slowly, Maya nodded. "But if he's catching a plane, he could be in Virginia in a couple of hours."

"Wasn't there a Florida town?" I asked. "Willinam, right?"

Maya nodded. "It's about an hour's drive from here. In the central part of the state."

"Maybe we should find a way to get there," I said.

"But we don't know if he's going there."

"At least we'd be doing *something*," I argued. "Isn't it worth a shot? We can't just sit here."

"But we can think of other stuff to do," Maya said. "Maybe we could try to find his credit card records. He could have charged a plane flight. Or maybe his secretary has a record of his trips. I haven't even had time to check his computer files yet. What if we go off on a wild-goose chase when we could be really accomplishing something here?"

"But he's going to firebomb another building!" I said.

"That's my point!" Maya said stubbornly. "We have to be careful. We have to *think*. We can't go off running half-cocked."

We sat in silence for a minute. Maya could be right. I just didn't know what to do.

"I wish I could remember the tones of the number he punched," Maya said. "That phone call could tell us everything."

I jackknifed to my feet. "It could!" I ran to the phone and looked at the buttons. My heart fell. Nothing was ever easy.

Then I had another idea. I dashed out of the office. Maya called after me, but I was too busy running to the reception area to answer.

I charged toward the phone. It was a different model from the one in the office, a newer one. Sure enough, there was a button saying LND—last number dialed.

I heard the sequence of tones as the phone redialed the number Yobel had punched in. Maya hurried in as the phone was ringing.

"What are you—"

I held up my hand. *"Shhhh."*

"Starlight Motel," said a voice with a deep Southern accent.

I don't know what I was expecting. But I wasn't expecting to get a motel. I deepened my voice.

"Ah, do you have any rooms available for tonight?"

"Sure do, sir. Would you like a double or two twin beds?"

"First, can you tell me exactly where you're located?"

"We're right off the interstate, exit twenty-two."

That wasn't very helpful. Which interstate? And which state? But wouldn't it look weird to ask?

"Now, what town are you in, exactly?" I asked.

"Kendal City," the voice answered promptly.

"Kendal City—what?"

"What?"

I rolled my eyes helplessly at Maya. "What, uh, *state*?"

Now the woman sounded wary. "Florida. Are you sure you want a room?"

"Florida," I repeated. Maya nodded slowly. "Are you anywhere near Willinam?" I asked.

"Next town over," the woman said. "Now, let me guess. You're going to the game, aren't you?"

"The game," I repeated.

"The state championship. I'm rooting for the Hayseeds, myself."

"The Hayseeds?"

"The Willinam High Hayseeds, darlin'. We are all big football fans over here. Now, let me quote you our rates. I've got a double room for—"

"Sorry, I changed my mind," I said. "I, um, don't like football."

I hung up the phone and turned to Maya. "Tell me something. Why do the Willinam Hayseeds sound so familiar?"

Maya grimaced. "Some Tornado fan you are."

Tornados was the name of our Bunnington Beach football team.

"So I'm not a football fan," I said.

"They're in the state championship," Maya told me. "And, come to think of it, they're meeting Willinam in the play-offs. Um, sometime this weekend, I guess. Wait a second. It's tonight!"

I sank into the desk chair. "Maybe that's why Yobel is going there. To see the game. Probably cover it for the station."

"Wait a second, Kincaid," Maya said. "He took the duffel bag, remember? Wouldn't reporting on the game be a great cover? He stays in the next town, just in case the FBI checks up on out-of-towners. But just in case they find him, he can always say that he went to Willinam for the big game."

"Bessamer, you have got a point," I said.

"We have to get there somehow," Maya said worriedly. "We have to warn them. We can call, but if they're anything like the rest of the police stations, they won't believe us."

"I know." I was thinking hard. "If the game is tonight, we could catch a ride. But it's probably too late. It's already past eight o'clock. Anybody who was going has gone by now."

"So what can we do?" Maya asked. "We can't ride our bikes all the way there."

"If we hurry, we can be right behind him," I said. "We could even beat him, if we're lucky."

"How, Randy?" Maya asked. "You're not thinking of stealing a car, are you?"

"Not technically," I said.

19//night riders

The moon was rising as Maya and I zoomed down the country road in my dad's BMW. We'd been on the road for forty minutes. More than halfway there.

My criminal skills were certainly improving. I was surprised how easy it had been to borrow my dad's pride and joy. Now a thirty-five-thousand-dollar masterpiece of German engineering was purring underneath my fingertips.

And I'd only stalled out three times getting out of town.

After we'd left SunBelt Comm, Maya and I had both headed back to our houses. Then we'd made this big show of yawning and saying how beat we were. We pretended to turn in early.

I already explained what night crawlers my parents were. That is, they crawled into bed before ten P.M. Tonight their favorite TV show was on at nine, and they usually watched it in bed with popcorn.

So it was a cinch to sneak down the stairs, lift my dad's keys, and hustle out to the garage. I left a note on my pillow explaining that the car wasn't stolen and that I'd have it back before midnight. But chances were that they'd never know it was gone.

Even with my parents' TV blaring, I didn't want to take chances. I opened the garage door manually instead of using the automatic opener, which makes a heck of a racket. Then I eased the car down the driveway in neutral. I didn't rev the engine until I was halfway down the block. My dad could probably pick out the sound of his particular motor from a half-mile away. Music to his ears.

I stalled a couple of times taking off from a stop sign on the way to Maya's. Then I stalled again as I pulled away from the corner where she was waiting for me. It was unfortunate. She gave me one of her looks.

"So I'm not so hot with a stick," I said. "Sue me."

"Just get us there in one piece," she said, making sure her seat belt was fastened.

Once we were out of Bunnington Beach, the four-lane road turned into a two-lane road, and the streetlights disappeared. My head-lights picked out asphalt and an occasional armadillo scurrying away into the brush.

Central Florida is a strange place. Spooky at night. You drive through pine forests, and then through scrub. The air smells swampy and feels thick against your skin. The towns are few and spread out. You can go for miles and miles without seeing another car.

Then, all of a sudden, the land turns hilly. There are curves in the road, and drops, and I had to really concentrate on my driving. It was still dark, and we were the only people on the road.

Maya moved toward me a fraction of an inch. "It's so dark out here," she said. "I'd hate to get stuck."

"Are you kidding? My dad tunes up the car about every five minutes," I said. "And it just looks spooky because it's so dark. During the day, you'd be all gushy, saying how awesome it is to be in the country, and how much fun it would be to live out here and have a horse and grow your own food. I know girls."

Maya gave me a cool look and then faced forward again. "I'm not like most girls."

I thought about this for a minute. Of course, I'd been saying it to myself ever since I met Maya Bessamer. But I'd been saying it in a negative way.

Maya isn't shy, but she isn't a flirt, either. She never flattered me. She isn't . . . soft. I'd never seen her out of jeans and a plain cotton shirt. But I could finally admit that Maya Bessamer has a certain appeal.

Because there is this way she smiles that makes you realize how pretty she is. And half the time when she zinged me, I had to force myself not to grin along with her.

Something had happened to me in Yobel's office. Maybe it was the way she had said, "I'm not leaving you here with him, Randy." She had been scared, but completely calm and determined. Something had happened to my heart right then.

Or take the time she put her hand in mine for a minute and squeezed it. That had just about made my knees buckle.

I spoke into the dark silence. "I know you're not like most girls," I said. "You're not like anyone."

I sneaked a look at her, and she looked back. It was dark in the car, but I could see her clearly. I felt like after only three days of being with her that I knew her face better than anybody's in the world. I knew all her expressions, and all her different ways of smiling.

But it turned out that I didn't. Because just

then Maya gave me a smile I'd never seen before. It was shy. Nice.

I had stolen my dad's precious car and was in the middle of nowhere, headed for a showdown with a killer. It was totally amazing, and probably stupid. But I felt like pulling the car over and kissing her, right then and there. Because my heart had just done this major pole-vaulting maneuver in my chest.

Then Maya turned to face the road again.

"Keep your eyes on the road, Kincaid," she said.

Her voice was cool and distant. And I wondered if I'd imagined that smile.

Just then, my headlights picked up a sign. WILLINAM 2 MILES.

I went around a curve and up a hill. A bridge loomed out of the darkness. When we got to the top, we could see the glow of Willinam up ahead.

I didn't have time to worry about smiles, and hearts that skip a beat. Things were about to get way serious. Way fast.

20//world on fire

Before we'd left, Maya had accessed the phone listing for Willinam. We'd looked up community centers, and we wrote down the address of the only one in town. We decided to go there first, then try the YMCA if it didn't pan out.

All we knew is that the target would be a place that catered to immigrants—or people the X Posse would consider non-Americans.

In a small town like Willinam, it wasn't hard to find your way around. I cruised down the dark, empty main drag and passed the bank, the post office, city hall, and the library.

"Where is everybody?" I asked. "This is spooky."

"They're all at the football game," Maya murmured. "Look."

Ahead, we could see a glow. I followed the light. Next to the tidy brick high school was a parking lot crammed with cars. Some of them were parked on the lawn. In back of the school, we could see the lighted football field. I cruised slowly past.

"I bet we're getting trounced," I said. "Look at those uniforms! So severely bogus."

Maya snorted. "It's halftime, bozo. That's a marching band."

The "Go Hayseeds" banner swung in the soft night air. One end of the field was decorated with about a hundred hay bales with a scarecrow perched on top. The band began to play "Old MacDonald."

"I don't know if I said this before, but I hate football," I said. I ground the gears as I drove past.

"Well, we know that the high school can't be the target," Maya said. "Just about everybody in the stands is white."

We crossed the railroad tracks and saw African Americans and Latin people out walking, or sitting on their stoops. Some young kids were playing in their front yard.

"Must be getting close," Maya murmured.

We cruised down one street after another. It only took a few minutes to find it.

PALMETTO PALM RECREATION CENTER

"This has got to be it," Maya said. "Oh, no," she breathed. She pointed to a sign:

STREET B-BALL EXHIBITION GAME TONIGHT.

We'd been hoping that the center would be dark and empty. But it was ablaze with light. People were hanging on the front steps, streaming in the doors, coming out again.

"Randy—"

"I know. Come on. There's no time to waste."

I pulled past the center and parked a block away, underneath a live oak tree. The car bumped over the roots as I pulled it way underneath the branches. The Spanish moss dripped down, hiding it from the street.

Suddenly, Maya gasped and clutched my arm.

"Look, Randy. Down the street, right near the center."

It was Yobel's van. I don't know how I could have missed it. It was parked under a broken streetlight.

A chill ran over me. "So he's here."

"He's here," Maya repeated. Her voice was flat.

"That means he's inside," I said.

"Planting the bomb," Maya said.

"So we still have time," I said. I turned to her. "Stay here with the car. I'm going to find someone in charge and try to convince them to evacuate the building."

She was already shaking her head as I finished. "No way, Kincaid. I'm going in with you.

You need me to help convince them. And you only saw Yobel once, across a parking lot, in the rain. You might not recognize him."

Now I was truly annoyed. "Maya, why should both of us be in danger? Stay here. That way you can tell the police if anything hap—"

Her face was set. "We don't have time for this, Kincaid. What is with you? Why are you trashing me now? Haven't I been there, shoulder to shoulder with you, all the way?"

Maya's dark eyes threw out sparks. She was right, as usual. She'd never backed down.

"Well, I wouldn't say shoulder to shoulder," I said. I measured out Maya's peanut height with my hand. "More like. . . shoulder to uh, hip."

Maya's grin flashed. "Big yuk. Let's go."

The sound of a basketball hitting the floor reached us as we hurried down the hall. Kids milled around, jostling each other and joking. They stared at us as we hurried by. We were the only white faces around. Talk about looking out of place.

But there was one consolation: Yobel would be easy to spot.

Maya must have had the same thought. "Why does he think he can get away with this?"

she murmured. "He'll stick out worse than John Tesh in a mosh pit."

We slipped into the gym. The noise was deafening. The kids on the gym floor weren't just playing basketball—they were putting on a show. And the crowd was loving it.

A referee taking a break stood against the wall, sipping a soda. She eyed us as she took a sip. She was short, with dark skin and red hair, and had the muscles of an athlete.

"Excuse me?" I yelled over the din. "Can you tell us where the person in charge is?"

She shrugged and made a circular motion with her finger to indicate the crowd. In other words, she had no idea.

Maya tugged at my shirt. "Come on."

Keeping to the back wall, we inched along until we had a good sight line into the standing-room-only crowd. They were just a blur of color and noise. It was hard to distinguish faces. I concentrated as hard as I could, but I hadn't really seen Yobel's face. It was up to Maya.

But no sooner did we find a place to stand than a group entered and spread out in front of us. I could still see, but Maya was too short.

She stood on her tiptoes, but it was no use. "Kincaid, I can't see!" she cried in frustration over the crowd's roar.

"Get on my shoulders," I suggested.

She hesitated. "Do you think that's such a good idea? I'll be too conspicuous. We want to see him, but we don't want him to see us."

It was a good point. Then again, Yobel might not even be in the stands. He could be anywhere. In the basement, or in one of the offices.

"Look, this is impossible anyway," I said in Maya's ear. "We'll never find him. We've got to look for the person in charge."

"Randy." Maya went suddenly still. She pressed back against the wall. "Randy, it's him."

"Where?"

Maya turned so that she faced me. "At the end of the bleachers to our right. Against the wall."

I followed Maya's gaze through the maze of arms and legs and saw him. Yobel was dressed as a security guard. He wore a blue uniform and had a baseball cap pulled low over his eyes and his hands in his pockets. He stood so still, he might have been a mannequin.

He was directly in our sight line. Which meant we were in his.

"Maya," I said in a low, urgent voice. "We have to move."

"I know," she said. "I can't! I'm trapped."

The crowd was too dense. They had shifted

back even farther, pressing against us. One of the players made a basket, and the people in front of us let out a roar.

Then one of the teenagers blew on some kind of noisemaker. The crowd had quieted by then, and the blare bounced off the tile wall.

I saw Yobel's eyes shift toward the sound. And then his gaze locked on Maya.

Her voice was soft, scared. "Kincaid . . ."

Yobel seemed frozen, just as we were. Then he started to move toward us. He had a clear field, and we were blocked in. All he had to do was grab us, and we were goners. Nobody would object to a security guard hustling two people out of the building. Or locking them in a basement while a bomb ticked away . . .

"Excuse me! Excuse me!" I pushed against the backs of the teenagers in front of us. But I only annoyed them. One of them turned, gave me a "don't mess with me" kind of stare, and turned back again. I pushed again. "Hey!" I said. "Let me through."

But he didn't let me through. He pushed back, hard. I hit the wall, and something hard pressed into my back.

A fire alarm.

Yobel was gaining. So I pulled it.

21//race against time

The alarm was piercing. It cut through the pandemonium like a shrill scream. Everyone stopped, even the players. There was a split second of silence.

And then came the screams. The overcrowded gym was suddenly a mass of pushing, shoving, panicked people.

I might have saved the crowd from a bomb, but what good would it do if people were crushed to death?

"Randy!" Maya's voice was frantic. She was being crushed against the wall.

I pushed and shoved until I was in front of her. Then I planted my hands against the wall and made my body as rigid as I could. I made a kind of cage, protecting her.

Maya began to cry. We'd been through so much, and this was the moment she picked to cry.

"I've got you safe," I said, murmuring close to her ear.

"I hate being small," she said fiercely through her tears.

"But you've got me," I said.

I turned my head to look for Yobel, but I couldn't see him through the pushing crowd. I did see a woman hurrying up the stairs at the end of the court. There was a room overlooking the gym with a big glass window. I watched as the woman ran inside.

In another few seconds, I heard a voice boom over the speaker system.

"Okay, brothers and sisters, take it easy, now. We can all get out safely, if you follow the drill. You can see the exits. Head toward the nearest one to you. Help your neighbor, now."

The voice was calm and strong. Slowly, the panic began to subside as the voice kept talking, directing, reassuring.

"There's no smoke, so we're not sure what's going on. But just keep walking, folks. That's right. You're doing fine. You help your neighbor, now."

I felt the pressure on my back ease. People were still trying to get to the exits, but they weren't shoving.

I kept Maya's hand in mine, and we let ourselves be absorbed in the stream of people, heading for the exit and the sweet night air.

We were carried down the hallway, and burst out the double doors to the front steps. We took big gulps of air as we hit the outside. People were milling around, not sure what to do or where to go.

"We'd better cross the street, just in case," I said to Maya.

I turned to a big group next to us. "If the boiler goes, the place could blow," I said. "I think we should cross the street."

The man nodded worriedly and started to herd his family across the street to a small playground. Luckily, others followed. At least if the bomb did go off, people wouldn't be milling right in front.

Keeping Maya's hand in mine, I pulled her over to stand by a palm tree. We stood behind a group of people wondering out loud whether to go home or stay to see if the game would continue.

The sound of sirens came to our ears. Seconds later, the engines pulled up, along with two police cars.

"At least we got everyone outside," Maya said. "That was a great idea, Kincaid."

"It's not over yet," I said.

"It might be," Maya said. "Look. There's Yobel. And the police are questioning him! Come on!"

I put a hand on her arm. "Wait."

"Why? We can tell them who he is! What he was going to do!"

But my eyes were on Yobel. I was watching his hand gestures. He was telling the cop something. And then he turned and pointed at me.

"Maya, walk away from me," I said. "Disappear into the crowd. *Now.* I'll meet you at the car if I can."

"Why?" she asked.

Why did the girl always have to argue?

"Because I think I'm about to be arrested," I said.

22//the fugitive

Maya melted away in the crowd as the police-man headed toward me. I knew it wouldn't do any good to run. I had to face Yobel down.

A meaty hand landed on my shoulder. It stayed there, like iron. The cop's frosty blue eyes seemed to bore right into me. The smile wasn't a smile.

"I hear you like pulling fire alarms, young man."

"Who told you that, officer?" I said. I used the Princeton voice.

"A security guard."

"Did you see his ID?" I asked.

The smile left the officer's face. "Seems like I'm the one who should be asking the questions around here. You from Willinam?"

I swallowed. "Bunnington Beach."

He let out a whistle. "You're a long way from home. Maybe you ought to come down with me to the station, and—"

"No!" I cried. The fingers tightened on my

shoulder, and I knew I was treading on thin ice. "What I mean is, officer," I said in a quiet voice, "that security guard isn't a security guard. I followed him here because he's involved in a conspiracy. All those firebombings you've been hearing about? He's one of those guys!"

The officer nodded. "Uh-huh."

I want to tell you, it's tough being a kid. Because nobody ever believes a word you say.

"If you'd just check his van," I said desperately, "you'd see—"

"Where's the girl?" The officer barked out the question.

My face went blank. "Girl?"

"He said there was a girl. Where is she?"

"I don't know what you're talking about," I said. "There's no—"

He pushed his face close to mine. "You're lying to me," he said softly. "And I'm getting mad, sonny. I just want you to know that."

Then I saw Maya. Instead of heading back to the car, she was standing just a few feet away.

"That guy said there was a bomb!" she cried in a surprisingly loud voice.

People looked around and stared, but nobody knew it was Maya who'd spoken. She's easy to overlook, and she'd melted back near the seesaws. Then her voice came from the direction of the swings. "Just like the community centers! We almost got blown up!"

Murmuring began. People looked around nervously.

This time, Maya's voice came from a different place. She stood smack in the middle of the sidewalk. And she pointed at Jeff Yobel.

"And that's the guy that did it!" she yelled. "Search his van!"

"Search his van!" someone else cried.

The officer's hand slipped off my shoulder. He peered through the crowd, trying to see Maya. Another officer headed for Yobel.

Yobel started to back away nonchalantly toward his van.

And then Maya took off. A teenager stood, looking over at Yobel, his sneakered foot resting lightly on his skateboard. With one deft movement, Maya kicked the skateboard out from under the kid and sent it shooting toward me.

All I had to do was jump, and the skateboard whizzed under my feet. On my downward jump, my feet hit the board, and I was off.

Bodies are no obstacles to a skateboarder. They're just fun things to whiz around. The referee who'd been drinking a soda earlier made a lunge for me, but I skirted her easily and she hit the dirt.

I made a quick half-circle around the water

fountain, then zoomed down the handicap ramp. I did a major ollie, flicking the board into the air right under my feet, over the remaining stairs to my right. I landed perfectly, right back on the board, and the momentum carried me out into the street.

It was all downhill from there. Literally. Willinam is one of the few hilly towns in Florida, and I lucked out. I flew past people, fire engines, and cop cars, straight toward freedom.

I went for blocks, until I was sure they hadn't followed me. Then I jumped off the skateboard. Keeping away from the streetlights, I started to circle back toward the car. I ran from shadow to shadow, being super careful.

I was starting to wonder if I should just head straight to the car when I saw Maya. She ran toward me. "I found you," she said. She could barely get the words out. She doubled over, trying to catch her breath.

"They're questioning Yobel," she said, panting.

"Are they going to arrest him?" I asked.

"Not sure," Maya said.

"Come on," I said. "Let's hide over here for a minute." We walked over to a lean-to shed that sheltered a bunch of garbage cans. We crammed ourselves inside, out of sight.

"They searched Yobel's van, and they didn't find anything," Maya said, breathing normally now. "The fire department is searching the center."

"So they could still bring me in, too," I said.

She nodded. A rustling sound came from one corner of the shed, and Maya jumped. "I'm trying not to think about rats right now," she muttered.

"There aren't any rats," I said. But I heard another rustle nearby, and Maya drifted closer to my shoulder.

"Kincaid?" Her voice was almost . . . timid.

"Yeah?"

"I was thinking . . . well, that maybe it's time to call our parents."

I didn't say anything, and Maya rushed on. "I mean, Yobel knows now that we told the police about him. He won't have access to a computer for a while, hopefully, so he won't be able to tell the rest of the X Posse what happened. Which gives the FBI time to nail the group without putting your family in danger. You know we won't be able to convince the FBI without our parents. We need adults. Adults who *know* us, I mean. Who know that we wouldn't make something this wild up. Who'll stand up to the cops and the

FBI and say that they believe their kid."

I snorted. "Maybe your parents will do that."

"Yes," Maya said quietly. "They will. And I think yours will, too. Randy, I know you're frustrated with your parents because you think they don't believe in you. That's what your whole airhead act is all about. You think they don't think you're smart."

"I don't think it," I said. "I know it."

"Well, I don't know if you're right or wrong," Maya said. "But here's the deal. It doesn't matter if you are. Because this whole thing is too important. Much more important than having problems with your parents. Don't you think so?" For a split second I was severely and seriously angry with Maya Bessamer for the first time in our relationship.

"Randy?" she said softly. "I just want to say something."

"I think you just said it," I said stiffly.

"I want to say," Maya went on, "that I think you're really smart."

I heard another rustle by a garbage can. I didn't flinch, but Maya jumped again. "And brave," she added. She gave me one of her stunner smiles.

I couldn't help grinning back at her. "Okay," I said. "You're right, as usual. But I won't hold it against you too much. Let's double back to the Beamer. I'll use the car phone."

We headed down the dark streets toward the car. Once a cop car passed us, but we hid behind a garage. We cut across a few back lawns.

The car was so hidden by the Spanish moss that you could barely see the gleam of the bumper. The cops had missed it, if they'd even known to look for it.

We waited a few seconds, just to make sure that the police—or Yobel—weren't around.

But the street was quiet. So we hurried over and ducked underneath the moss.

Just as I was putting the key into the lock, a car pulled up to the curb. The headlights shone right on us.

A friendly voice called out, "Randy? Maya? Is that you?"

I turned. It was Mr. Pogue, of all people.

"Mr. Pogue! What are you doing here?"

He leaned out of the car window. "I'm lost, that's what I'm doing here. I drove the Chess Club over to see the big game at Willinam High. They sent me out for burgers, and I can't find my way back to the high school." He wagged a bulging bag at us. "Getting tempted to eat these myself. You know that French fry smell that you just can't resist?"

"Sure, Mr. Pogue," I said.

"You lost, too?"

"No," I said. "I can lead you back to the high school, if you want."

"Fantastic!"

I opened the car door. Maya slid into the passenger seat.

"That's funny," I said. "Mr. Pogue didn't even notice that I shouldn't be driving."

"We should tell him about this," Maya said.

"Mr. Pogue?" I turned on the car and started to back out. "He's a loser."

"So what? He's an adult who knows us. We could ask him to go to the police station with us. Call our parents. He'd help!"

"I guess," I said, pulling out into the street.

The car phone suddenly rang. "Oh, no," I breathed. "It's my dad. He found out about the car."

"So answer it," Maya said in that logical voice that could drive Mr. Spock up a wall. "You said you were going to call him, anyway."

I picked it up. "Hello?"

"Randy? It's me. Mr. Pogue."

"Mr. Pogue? How did you get—"

"I just want to tell you, Randy. A word to the wise. There's a stop sign ahead. I advise you to go through it."

I rolled my eyes at Maya. Mr. Pogue was making a lame joke, as usual. "We're not in driver's ed now, Mr. Pogue. I'll stop."

"Well, it's up to you, I guess," Mr. Pogue said. "But the thing is, if you hit the brakes, Randy, your car will blow up."

He sounded so calm. It took me a minute to make sense of what Mr. Pogue said. "That's not funny," I said.

"Oh, I think it's a riot." Mr. Pogue giggled. "And I think you kids deserve it, too. Did you really think you could catch us? We're so much bigger. And we're *right*. We're patriots."

"Patriot," I whispered. The car was picking up speed, and I took my foot off the gas.

"Oh, I wouldn't do that, either," Mr. Pogue said. "You don't want to stall out. Boom!"

I put my foot on the gas again, and the car leaped forward.

"What are you *doing*?" Maya asked crossly.

"I know what a terrible driver you are, Randy," Mr. Pogue said. "No concentration. I don't expect you to make it past the town line. So I guess I'll say good-bye now."

"You can't do this! Mr. Pogue!"

"Oh, by the way. You got a D in history."

And then I heard a click.

23//pedal to the metal

It wasn't a movie. It was real. My hands were slick as they grabbed the wheel. Mr. Pogue passed us, waving, and zoomed off into the night.

"What's going on?" Maya asked, clutching the door handle.

"Pogue is Patriot," I said. "He rigged the car. He just told me that if I step on the brake, or stall, it'll blow up."

"No!" Maya shouted. "No! This can't be happening."

"I think it is," I said. "He sounded serious. Crazy."

It was after eleven P.M. now. People must go to bed early in Willinam, because the streets were quiet. Which was lucky for me. I had to go through every stop sign I saw.

I knew I had to slow down. But downshifting would be my undoing. That's when I'd stall out.

I had to do it. "Hang on," I said.

I downshifted into third. The car lurched, and the speed dropped.

"Can we drive until we run out of gas?" Maya asked. Fear vibrated through her voice, but I could tell she was trying to be calm.

"We've got half a tank," I said, glancing at the gauge. "I can't drive that long without having to brake."

I ran through another stop sign. I just hoped the cops weren't still around. If they went after me in a high-speed chase, I'd lose it for sure. Mr. Pogue was right about one major thing: I was a lousy driver.

"We don't know if that would work, anyway," Maya said. "It would be the same as stalling, wouldn't it? The car might blow up."

I wiped the sweat off my forehead. "Good point."

We flashed past dark houses, dark streets.

"Randy!" Maya cried. "This is a dead end!"

The end of the street loomed ahead. A bunch of trees and a huge garbage Dumpster.

I turned the wheel and the car lurched, throwing Maya against the door. It bumped over a curb, and I had to give it gas so that it wouldn't stall. Then I drove across someone's front yard, skirted a small rubber swimming pool, and bumped back down on the road in the opposite direction.

"We can't keep doing this," Maya said frantically. "We've got to get out of town. We're going to crash into something."

"But which way is out of town? I'm all turned around now."

"I think if we go straight, we'll hit that main road again," Maya said. "You'll have to make a tight turn, though."

We sped through the streets. The moon was high and full. I wondered if it was the last time I'd see it.

"The turn is coming up," Maya said. "At the corner."

"Hang on," I said. I downshifted again. The car shuddered and lurched, but I kept my foot on the gas, and it didn't stall. My hands were slick with sweat as I turned the wheel. The tires squealed, but we made it safely.

Now I could head straight past the high school and be out of town in just a few minutes. Especially at this speed.

But what then? We'd be on a dark country road, miles from anywhere. The car would eventually run out of gas. Or I'd have to brake to negotiate a curve.

Then I remembered the bridge outside of town. The road curved sharply on the approach.

There was a concrete wall on one side. On the other, a deep ditch filled with water.

We'd never make it.

Maya didn't remember the bridge. I could see that. All she remembered was the miles of straight road. Her body was pressed back against the seat, as if she could slow down the car by her body weight. She was terrified.

I couldn't tell her we were heading for disaster.

The high school was just ahead. All the lights were off. The game was over. I wondered for a second who won. I could see the "Hayseed" banner, still waving in the wind.

In a minute we'd be past it.

"Maya," I said. "Unhook your seat belt."

Her hands fumbled at the catch. "What are you going to do?"

"I'm going to stop the car. But before it stops, we're going to jump out."

She nodded at me, her eyes wide.

"It's the only way. You have to jump clear of the car. Keep your knees bent, and roll. Keep rolling. Don't stop. Can you do that?"

"Yes," she said. "Yes, Randy. I can do that. But how are you going to stop the car without brakes?"

I made a sharp turn into the high school

parking lot. I had to gun the motor to make it over the curb. I bumped along the grass. Dirt flew and branches cracked as we drove over the ground.

Unhooking my seat belt, I headed toward the football field. The bleachers lined two sides. As we flew down the field, I downshifted again. I was getting the hang of it now. I knew the car wouldn't stall, and it didn't. It slowed. I was able to keep it at that speed without braking. But we were still going too fast to jump out. I headed for the end zone. I drove right through the goal.

Maya saw the hay bales and the huge haystack ahead. Her voice trembled. "Randy?"

"Get ready. I'll count to three. Jump on three."

"On three," she repeated, her voice shaking.

I had to hit the bales just enough to slow down the car, not stall it out. I had to work the shift and the gas, and never touch the brake. I couldn't stall. I had to find the perfect place to jump, a place where Maya could roll on a soft bed of hay, instead of hard ground. And the car had to stall out a good distance away from us, so we wouldn't get caught in the blast.

All these things clicked away in my head clearly. It was like time slowed down. I knew what I was going to do. I saw my opening. And I was ready to risk it.

The car bumped along the hay bales. I downshifted again. Here, hay was spread in a thick carpet over the grass.

"One," I said.

The car hit a hay bale. It shuddered. I shifted and heard the gears grind. I had to give it a little gas.

"Two. Open your door!"

I let off the gas again. The car slowed down. Maya and I both opened our doors. We gave each other one last, desperate look. Then I nodded at her, and she nodded back.

"Three. Jump!"

24//last chance

I caught the flash of Maya's white shirt as she jumped. It was harder for me, having the steering wheel there. I didn't get as clear as I wanted. I kind of fell out backward, and I felt a sharp pain in my shoulder. But the hay was a good cushion. I rolled, and kept on rolling.

The car burst through the haystack, rolled forward to the wall of a shed, and stalled out. A split second later, it blew up.

So Pogue wasn't lying.

Black smoke billowed out toward us, carried by the wind, and I crawled over to where Maya still lay. My heart stopped. She wasn't moving.

"Maya!" I called. "Maya!"

I crawled next to her. I was afraid to touch her, so I touched her hair. She moaned.

"Are you all right?"

"I'm okay. I think."

Her face was against the hay, and I brushed the hair off her cheek. "What are you doing?"

Her voice was muffled. "Kissing the ground."

I laughed, and I felt a twinge in my shoulder. Maya instantly sat up.

"Randy! You're hurt!"

"Just a scratch," I said. I rotated my shoulder carefully. "It's my shoulder. I think it's just bruised. We were lucky."

Maya looked over at the burning car. Her expression was sober. "Yes. Very lucky."

"Come on," I said. "We'd better put a call in to the fire department before the whole school burns down."

We walked across the field, toward the main street. We looked for a phone. But within a few minutes, we could hear the sirens. It was a big night for the Willinam FD.

Maya pulled me down a side street. "We have to talk," she said. "The police can't see you, Randy. Not yet. You're already in trouble for pulling that fire alarm. What are they going to think if they see a burned-out car? They could hold us here for hours, and we'd never get to the FBI."

"I see your point," I said. I must have been in some kind of shock-type thing, because I hadn't thought about what would happen if the police saw me. I hadn't thought about how to get home. I hadn't thought about what to do next. I was just so glad that we were alive.

Suddenly, Maya sank down on the front lawn of somebody's white frame house. "I'm beat, Randy," she said. "We have to find a phone so I can call my parents." When she looked up at me, her eyes glittered with tears. "Please?"

My heart felt like somebody was wringing it out like a mop. I sat down next to her. "Of course," I said. "That's what we decided to do, remember? The car bomb distracted us."

A smile flitted across her face. "Some distraction."

"Yeah, well, now we're smokin'."

Maya poked me. "Don't use that word, will you?"

We laughed together, really softly. I began to think that maybe we'd get out of this.

Then a dark green Escort pulled up by the curb. Mr. Pogue leaned out the window.

"Hey, kids. Surprise! I didn't expect to see you again."

The fear that had been tucked down underneath relief suddenly roared to life.

I eyed Mr. Pogue. Maya was stiff beside me. We'd have to outrun him.

"Don't even think about running," Mr. Pogue said. "You can't outrun a car."

"Who are you kidding?" I said. "It's an Escort."

I don't know how I had the nerve to joke. But being angry helped keep the fear tamped down.

"Spoiled kid," Mr. Pogue said pleasantly. "You're all spoiled kids. They should pay me double." He nodded toward the backseat. "Get in."

Maya and I hesitated. Should we run? What if he had a gun?

"I'm getting im-pat-ient," Mr. Pogue sang out teasingly. The sound sent chills through me, and I felt Maya shiver.

"And I have a bo-mb," Mr. Pogue continued. He held up a small canvas tote bag. "Catch!"

Maya screamed as Mr. Pogue feinted a throw. His face contorted. "That's not nice, Maya. Noisy. Now get in. Fast."

We didn't have a choice. From the look in Mr. Pogue's eyes, I knew he'd kill himself along with us if he had to. So we got in the backseat, and Mr. Pogue sped away.

"Didn't think you had it in you, Randy," he said. "I was waiting at that curve by the bridge, and you never showed up. Could have knocked me over with a feather."

"Where are you taking us?" Maya asked.

"Don't mind telling you, you kids have been getting on my nerves," Mr. Pogue said. "Yobel and I knew someone was on our tail, but we never thought it was a couple of kids. Let alone some of my own students." His chuckle belonged in a straitjacket. "Didn't think any of you were smart enough."

Mr. Pogue turned off the main road.

I repeated Maya's question. "Where are you taking us?"

"Yobel is no whiz kid, either," Mr. Pogue went on. "But he's an Einstein compared to JamminGuy. It's a wonder I was able to coordinate all those dunderheads. But all you need is one genius at the head."

"Who's that, Mr. Pogue?" I asked in a fake-innocent voice.

"You can't rile me, Randy," Mr. Pogue said. "Know why? I see you coming from a mile away. Unlike you, my IQ is in the triple digits."

Now I ask you. Is that fair? The guy was planning to blow me to smithereens, probably, and he had to insult me, too?

Then Maya piped up. "Oh, is that why you were voted Mr. Snoresville of Bunnington Beach High? At least people don't fall asleep while Randy is talking."

"I don't know why they ever let you in the country," Mr. Pogue snarled. Tires squealed as he made the turn.

"Maybe because I was born here," Maya shot back.

"Well, you're not an American, Little Miss Chopsticks," Mr. Pogue muttered.

I saw Maya's face flush. But she didn't back down. "Remind me to show you my birth certificate," she snapped.

"I don't think we'll be meeting again," Mr. Pogue said.

My nerves were screaming as Mr. Pogue turned down another dark street. I kept eyeing the brown tote bag on the front seat. It didn't seem to make sense to grab it and run, since it might blow up. And Mr. Pogue was driving too fast for Maya and me to try the same roll-out maneuver.

And then I noticed that the street we were on looked familiar. "Where are you taking us?" I asked again.

Mr. Pogue grinned. "Thought you'd want to see the end of the game."

Maya and I exchanged uneasy glances. Mr. Pogue pulled up across the street from the community center. The lights were still burning.

"Actually, you did us a favor earlier," he said, staring at the building. "Set a false alarm, have the fire department check the building. Then everybody goes back in to finish the game. Plus,

I got rid of Yobel. That guy was starting to get on my nerves. He's down at the police station. He thinks I'm back home, waiting to hear how he did. But I didn't trust him to pull this one off—not after he messed up at the diner. I trusted him on that job. And it was my own personal choice. I used to go there when I was a kid. Before Bunnington Beach was ruined."

"Mr. Pogue, why don't you let us go?" Maya said. "The cops don't have anything on you yet."

"Are you kidding? Yobel is probably singing his brains out right now. I've got nothing to lose. Tonight, I'm going out with a bang."

He turned in the seat and grinned at us. The light from a streetlight hit his eyes. The funny thing is, he didn't look crazy. He looked like Mr. Pogue. Kind of nerdy, kind of pompous, kind of sad.

"You mean you're going to try to set off the bomb again?" Maya asked in a small voice.

He picked up the canvas tote. "It's going to be glorious. A regular Fourth of July." He grinned at us. Now he did look crazy. "Don't you want to be part of it?"

25//smithereens

He locked us in the office overlooking the gym. But first, he ripped out the phone. Then he unscrewed all the lightbulbs and smashed them. He checked the closets for more, and smashed them, too.

It was dark in the office, but there was a glass window overlooking the brightly lit gym. We could see the players and the cheering people in the bleachers. It wasn't as packed as before, just about half full.

We could see them, but they couldn't see us. We could even hear them faintly. But they couldn't hear us. The plate glass was thick.

"Don't even think about trying to break it," he said. "It's unbreakable glass."

He put the bag in a corner. He set the timer for seven minutes.

"Want to catch some of the game before I leave," he said. "I like to look at the faces. I want to remember them in my dreams.

This way, you can watch them, too."

"You're crazy," Maya said. Her voice shook with fear and contempt.

"I'm right, Chopsticks," Mr. Pogue answered, unconcerned. "That gives me power. I'm leading us toward a free America."

"You're sick!" Maya yelled, but he was already shutting the door and locking it. She banged on it with her fists. "You're out of your mind!"

We only heard his footsteps walking away.

I checked out the office. I pounded on the glass window, but no one would hear me, not up this high. I tried the door, but it was heavy oak, and locked tight.

"Stand back," I told Maya. I picked up a desk chair and smashed it against the window. I felt the impact shudder up my bones, and a jolt of pain traveled from my shoulder down my arm.

The glass didn't break. Didn't even crack.

"It's hopeless," Maya said. She stood looking out at the crowd. "Hopeless," she whispered.

"Stand back," I said. I hit the glass with the chair. It bounced off harmlessly as my shoulder screamed in protest.

She retreated to the other wall of the office. Her eyes stayed on the bomb.

"Come here," I said. I held out my hand, and she took it. I squeezed her hand. "We're going to get out of here."

"I wish we could leave a note or something," Maya said, as if she hadn't heard what I'd said. "Something that will survive—"

She stopped, swallowing. *Because we won't,* we were both thinking.

"—the blast, so that they'd know who did it."

"Maya, we're going to get out of this," I said. "*We'll* tell them all about Pogue."

Maya's eyes darted around the office, moving from the bomb to the clock.

"Maya," I said. "Listen to me, okay? We have to think."

"I should have known," she said. "I worked on his computer, Randy! But I did it for free. He just wanted to back up his hard drive. It was such a little job. I didn't put him in my client files. But I should have remembered!"

"Maya, it's okay," I said. "It doesn't matter now. It's okay," I said soothingly.

Maya nodded rapidly. She licked her lips. "Okay. Okay, then."

"Okay," I said.

Six minutes to go.

Six minutes to think. Or not to think. Not to

think about an explosion, about fire and smoke and being blown through a wall.

Not to think about glass too strong to shatter, a door too thick to break down.

I tried once more to break the glass. Using every ounce of strength, I smashed the chair against it. It bounced off. Then Maya tried. She could barely lift the heavy oak chair, so she used a brass lamp. It broke, but the window stayed intact.

She beat on it with her fists. We both screamed. But the game went on. Nobody noticed a thing.

"They can't see us," she said. "Or hear us. And we can't warn them." She pressed her forehead against the glass. "They can't hear a thing."

And that's when I knew we weren't going to get out.

The same knowledge was in Maya's dark eyes. "Maybe we should get under the desk," she said in a small voice. "It might . . . help when it happens. Plus I can't stand to see the clock, Randy."

Five minutes to go.

Hand in hand, we walked to the battered wood desk. Papers were stacked neatly on the blotter. A file read DAY CARE and another, BUDGET

A paper set squarely in the center was headed
MONDAY A.M. ANNOUNCEMENTS.

Also on the desk was one of those photo
frames that opened out with three pictures in it.
In the middle frame, a family stood in their
Sunday best. Surrounding the photo were two
others. One was of a boy about ten years old,
with chocolate brown eyes and a goofy grin.
The other was of the older son, dressed in a basketball uniform. He was tall and looked as
though he had a mean hook shot. The name-
plate on the desk read: DOMINIQUE LAGUERRE.

"I wonder if she's down in the gym," Maya
said. She delicately touched the first photo.
"Nice family."

We slid under the desk, still holding hands.
We sat very close together.

"I didn't really like you at first, you know,"
Maya said. "I mean, I thought you were some
surfer dude who didn't care about things. Didn't
think about things. I guess I gave you a hard
time."

"I gave you one, too," I said.

"Yeah," Maya said. "You did."

"But I think you're radical," I said. "A
severely turbocharged babe."

I was trying to make her smile, and she did.
"Thanks."

We were quiet for a minute. I tried to figure out how much time was left.

Four and a half minutes, maybe a few seconds more. Would it seem long? I hoped so.

It was hard in the small place, but I put my arm around Maya. I thought about all the laughing, cheering people in the gym. How could someone hate so much that they could smash all that life?

Those people didn't have a chance. None of us had a chance. Even now, it was too late. There wouldn't be time to get everyone out in the orderly way they'd exited earlier. I wondered if the tall woman who'd run up the stairs and spoken so calmly had been Dominique LaGuerre.

I sat up and banged my head against the top of the desk. "PA," I said.

"What?" Maya asked.

But I was wiggling out from underneath the desk, fast and awkwardly, trying to get to my feet.

"There's a PA system in here, Maya!" I said. "There's got to be. Remember before, in the gym, when the voice was telling people to be calm? And here"—I shook the paper at her—"Monday announcements!"

"But where?" Maya asked, standing up and

looking around wildly. "I don't see it!"

I flung open the closet door, but it was filled with paper and office supplies.

"Here, Randy!" Maya had swung open the door of a battered metal cabinet.

A microphone rested on a console. The thing looked about a million years old. I prayed I could make it work. I flipped the switch. A light glowed red.

"Hurry, Randy," Maya breathed. "Only four minutes left."

I blew into the PA. But of course, I couldn't tell if I was transmitting. I covered the microphone. "Maya, go to the window," I said. "Tell me if I'm getting through."

She sped over to the window. I took my hand off the mike.

"Attention, people," I said. I reminded myself to speak slowly and distinctly. "Attention! There has been a bomb scare in the building. You must evacuate as quickly as possible and in an orderly fashion."

"They stopped playing," Maya said. "They're listening. Or booing. Or something. They don't believe you, Randy. They think it's another false alarm!"

"This is not a drill," I said. "Repeat, this is not a drill! It's a bomb scare. Everyone move toward the exits! Now!"

"It's Pogue!" Maya said shrilly. "He's heading out of the gym! He's coming for us, Randy!"

"The person who set the bomb is in the building," I said. "He's middle-aged and has brown hair—oh, and he's white! Hold him! And get out as quickly as you can."

"I can't see," Maya said. "I can't tell if they caught him."

Three minutes left.

"Just keep moving! And can somebody come to the office and—"

The door shuddered. Someone was trying to break it down. It shuddered again.

And then the muscular referee with the red hair burst into the office. She was followed by another ref and two more men dressed casually in jeans.

"FBI," she said. "Where's the bomb?"

I pointed to the corner. "Three minutes left," I said.

"Then you'd better get moving," she answered. "Feeney!" she barked.

Another referee appeared. He grabbed my arm and Maya's and hustled us out of the office and down the hall. Running, we sprinted for the exit. "What about her?" I asked as we ran. "Did you bring the bomb squad?"

"Vorshack *is* the bomb squad," Feeney replied.

It was all over pretty quickly. Pogue was surrounded by the kind of people he hated. They held him until the FBI found him.

The agents had Pogue handcuffed and spread-eagled against a car in about two seconds.

"I am a citizen of the United States of America!" he shouted.

"You are a deranged crank," Maya said.

The police kept us back, across the street, but within a few minutes we heard that Agent Vorshack had dearmed the bomb. She'd been the agent I'd been transferred to at the FBI. Can I pick 'em, or what?

And Dominique LaGuerre pushed through the crowd, looking for "the boy on the PA." She asked to shake our hands, and thanked us for saving the day.

I wouldn't say the FBI was as cuddly, though. They were mighty ticked off that Maya and I had done so much on our own. And the first thing they did was call our parents. Then Vorshack assigned an agent to watch us and warned us not to move until she was ready for us. She meant it. For once, Maya and I obeyed orders.

So it wasn't as though we got the credit that we so obviously deserved. But Maya and I felt pretty good, anyway. We watched the FBI drive Mr. Pogue away.

"It's finally over," I said.

Maya nodded. She slung her arm around me, which wasn't easy, considering our height difference.

"I am severely stoked," she said.

//epilogue

It took the FBI hours to download all the info from our brains into theirs. It turned out that our warnings to all the towns beginning with "Willi" actually did some good. They traced the calls to Yobel's phone. While Maya and I were driving, the bureau was on the move. They are way cool.

Agent Vorshack had already been on the case. She'd even bought a copy of *Johnny Tremain*! It turned out that the FBI had already figured out that the bomb in the diner had used some kind of solvent that dry cleaners use. So when Agent Vorshack heard about Yobel, everything clicked.

Of course, they were just as clueless as we were when it came to Mr. Pogue. They arrested Yobel, but he didn't betray Pogue after all. He said he had acted alone, and he wanted his lawyer. But Agent Vorshack decided that it might be a good idea to stick around. Something didn't feel right, she said. She has severely excellent intuition, if you ask me. And it saved our lives.

It took them a couple of weeks to round up all the rest of the members of the X Posse. They were spread all over the country. JamminGuy lived in Nebraska. SwampFox was in South Carolina. And he was a man! They were all arrested for federal conspiracy crimes.

And Mr. Pogue turned out to be a radically bad dude. He had major explosives stored all over his house. In peaceful old Bunnington Beach.

Agent Vorshack called to tell me that Pogue had finally spilled the rest of the code. After PAT.riot73 would say, "Time to . . ." the next word would contain the first three letters of the state the target was in. As in, "Time to tend to my business . . ." equals Tennessee. And, "Time to misplace my glasses . . ." referred to Mississippi.

I said I felt totally stupid to not have figured out something so easy. But Agent Vorshack told me not to sweat it. She didn't figure it out, either. And neither did any of their crack code breakers. Of course, they all thought Vorshack had hold of a crackpot idea.

Anyway, Maya and I were major media stars

for a few days. Some Hollywood guy even called, asking me for the rights to my story. I was pretty full of myself for a while, but Maya kept making fun of me and calling me "Superstar," so I quit.

Can you beat this, though? I actually got grounded for taking my dad's car! Talk about bad behavior! Parents are the worst. I solve a national terrorist conspiracy, and I get punished. My parents said I should have come to them when things got hairy. Never mind that they never would have believed me.

But they also said they were proud of me. Here's the strange part: My dad said he wasn't surprised. He said that between me and a criminal mastermind, he'd bet on me any day. He might have been snowing me—in fact, I know he was—but it still felt good.

Normally, I would have gone completely ballistic about being grounded, but the truth was, I didn't mind hanging at home for a few days. Feeling safe. And now that I had my laptop, I could talk to Maya as much as I wanted. And I got to say things to her that I never would have been able to say in person.

Which is how I became one of those dudes following the prettiest four-eyed cybergeek around. Heartbreaker? You bet. She could break your heart just by standing in front of you.

But how's this for luck? Even with those cute glasses, the girl can't see straight. Because she told me—she actually likes me best.

Talk about stoked!

A **SNEAK PREVIEW** OF THE NEXT
SUSPENSE-FILLED RIDE DOWN THE
INFORMATION SUPERHIGHWAY!

danger.com

@3//Shadow Man/

b y
jordan.cray

9//the sound and the fury

Just then, a crowd of tourists appeared at the top of the ladder. The man dropped the gun and stuck his hand in his pocket.

"Don't move," he growled.

"But you just told us to move," Nick said. "Now I'm totally confused."

"Shut up, kid," the man said warningly.

The tourists were a noisy bunch. They called out things like "Just look at that rigging!" and, "Let's see you climb that mast, Bob!" They started to move in our direction. I was never so glad to see a bunch of chatty, obnoxious people in my life.

"Okay, this is what we're going to do," the man said calmly. "You're going to walk in front of me slowly. We're going to go down that ladder, and straight to the parking lot. Got it?" He jerked his head toward the ladder at the opposite end of the deck.

What could we do? Looking into his cold

gray eyes, I had no doubt that he would shoot us right here, if he had to. And then he would use the confusion to melt away.

Suddenly, Nick started talking in a loud voice.

"Aye, sir, yes, sir, let's move along," he shouted. "The cap'n likes us hale and hearty, and quick on our feet!"

What was he talking about? The man looked confused, and I was just as clueless.

"The name's Ethan Hobbledehoy, and I first shipped out at the tender age of eleven," Nick shouted.

The families overheard him, and started toward us. A man nudged his wife.

"Honey, get the kids," he said. "They should hear this."

"Where's Timmy?" a woman cried. "Timmy!"

"I served under the fiercest cap'n of all, mateys, Cap'n Jack Howdy," Nick called out.

Blame my state of terror, but it took me this long to figure out that Nick was pretending to give a lecture. All the tourists figured he was one of the Mystic Seaport employees who stay in character as whalers, or smithys, or whatever nineteenth-century type jobs were.

Suddenly, cameras clicked, and video cameras were trained on Nick. Our man looked panicked, and he started to edge away.

"I can't see!" a kid cried.

"Here, Timmy," the woman said, lifting him.

"He ended up at the bottom of the sea, they say," Nick said, eyeing our man. "Some say because he was so cruel and dog-ugly," Nick added, with a lift of the eyebrow at him. "Whippin's and keenhaulin's—I saw them all."

Timmy brightened at the thought of mayhem and torture, and the crowd pressed closer with their cameras. Our man, with a last furious look at us, faded back.

I saw a security guard hit the deck. I signaled Nick—or should I say Ethan Hobbledehoy—with my eyes.

Nick grabbed my hand. "Then I met Flossie here. We opened a chandler's shop down below. Come and join us!"

Nick tugged my hand, and we hurried toward the stairs. Most of the crowd followed us, and the security guard was trapped in the middle of them.

Nick and I didn't wait to see what happened to our man, or the security guard, or even little Timmy. We ran.

We didn't stop running until we reached the

parking lot. We leaped in the car and locked all the doors. I gunned the motor and took off toward the ferry.

"Is anybody following us?" I asked.

Nick searched the traffic behind us. "I don't think so."

"By the way, it's *keel*hauling, not *keen*hauling," I said.

"Yeah? Well, I just love those *cactus-* scented candles," Nick said.

We both burst out laughing. We laughed a little too long, so I knew Nick was probably as close to hysteria as I was.

We had a reservation, so we made it onto the noon ferry. We got cups of hot chocolate and stood outside on the deck, watching the line of cars inch forward. If you didn't make a reservation, you had to wait to see if you could get on. I felt comforted, just looking at the routine I knew so well.

"That was way close," I said. The hot chocolate tasted so hot, and so good.

"Look, I never figured it would turn out that way," Nick said. "I'm sorry, Annie."

I didn't think Nick was capable of an apology.

"It wasn't your fault," I said, even though it kind of was. "And Nick?"

He was scanning the parking lot. "Yeah?"

"I'm sorry I called you a plastic Hefty bag."

"It's okay," he said. "I shouldn't have called Josh a Samsonsite."

I turned my back to the dock and leaned against the rail. I used the cup to warm my hands. "Did you ever see a gun before?"

Nick shook his head. "I could have done without seeing it this time."

"You were masterful," I said. "That speech was incredible. But tell me something. What's a chandler?"

Nick grinned. "Search me. It just floated into my head."

Suddenly, Nick's grin froze. He stared at something over my shoulder.

"What is it?" I asked.

"Annie, look," he said softly. He grabbed my sleeve and pulled me away from the rail, into the shadow of the overhanging top deck. "The station wagon. Isn't that him?"

Down below, a man was leaning against the passenger door of a dark blue station wagon. He was wearing a baseball cap. He looked up at the ferry and stared straight at us. He waved.

"It's him," I said.

"He must have followed us," Nick said. I saw him swallow.

"He's on the no-reservation line," I said.

"Maybe he won't make it on."

For the next ten minutes, we watched as car after car was directed to drive onto the ferry. The dark blue station wagon inched forward in the line.

"He's going to make it," Nick said grimly.

"We've got to hide!" I said. But I knew the ferry inside and out. There weren't that many places to hide. He'd find us eventually.

But just then, I heard a clanging noise. It was harsh and grating, but it sounded sweet to my ears.

"They're closing it up!" I cried. "He didn't make it onboard!"

Nick slumped against the rail in relief. The ferry's engines revved, and the man pulled out of the line and headed for the exit.

"We're safe," I said.

Nick's dark eyes were worried when he turned to me. "For now," he said. "But Annie, he knows we're from Scull Island. How long will it take him to find us?"